PZ4
D26165Co

DATE DUE			
JUL 9 '79			
		WITHDRAWN	

COMING HOME

Random House | New York

COMING HOME

George Davis

To Maryesther,
Pam and Chris

When men of wealth urge the use and show of force . . . then it is to protect a little spot of private security against the resentful millions from whom they have filched it . . .
—Richard Wright, *Native Son*

THAILAND

Stacy...

I come into the red wooden showerhouse. It is up on piles to keep snakes—cobras, vipers—from crawling up the drains.

Childress is there already with the water coming down over his head. Above the roar of the water, he says, "I'm not gon' let a Harvard-trained nigger inherit the best whore in Thailand."

I repeat it: "So you're not . . ." I say. I don't want to say nigger because I don't know if he'd like hearing a white person say it. I drop my shower clogs out the door into the sand.

"I don't think I will," he says. The water is coming down over him, beating the top of his head, pulling the curls out of his slightly Negroid hair. He opens his mouth and lets water flow into it.

"Why?"

"I don't know," he says. He stops soaping himself and stares for a moment. "I don't know."

I watch him and say to myself: Why, if you're back in America and don't give a damn about Thailand or Ben or the Vietnam war? I watch the clear water flow across his brown skin. He soaps himself, and then he stands and lets the water wash the soap downward into the drain on the floor.

He gets out of the shower and starts to dry himself on a large green towel. I come out and down the stairs too. He must have been in the shower a long time before I woke up, I think. His brown skin is a little grayish from all the water that has run over it. Grayish like his mouth is sometimes when he comes down from flying and takes his oxygen mask off. Gray and greaseless.

"She's been with me six months," he says. "For some reason it wouldn't feel right, him having her."

"So you got a way to stop him?" I ask.

"No. But I'll think of something before I go."

"You'd better dry off. We only got fifteen minutes."

"What time's briefing?"

"Thirteen past. You wouldn't want to be late for your last run."

"Yeah, got to go kill my last Gook."

I stare at him as he continues to dry himself. He is heavy but muscular. His toes are curled up to keep them out of the sand.

"You or Ben in my flight?" he asks.

"No, Ben's earlier and I'm a half-hour later."

"Too bad, I'd like one of you to see-me-do-it this one last time."

I start across the sand, walking along a path which sep-arates the beach from the reedy jungle. The towel hangs around my waist. Dozens of pilots come out of their tents and out of the other small raised showerhouses. Childress follows me along the path.

Ben...

A dump truck wakes me. Noisily the truck plows along the dusty road beside the tent. Another truck follows. I open one eye and watch them through the screen at the side of the tent. The wheels pick up dust and throw it off like water off the prow of a boat. Soon they will finish the new runways they are building down near the gulf, I think.

Stacy's and Childress' cots are empty. I think about Childress singing in the shower. I think about this being his last mission, and about me getting his girl, Damg, after he goes back to the States. I push myself deep into the mattress on my cot. Eighty more missions for me. Twenty gone. I wonder how many people I have killed. I never think about killing unless I consciously decide to think about it. Childress must never think about it. I must be more lost than he is, more self-divided, or maybe he's more self-divided than me.

I pull myself out of the bed and smother my face in my hands, trying to seal my nose from some of the dust that the sun seems to beat out of the canvas tent-top. Already the day is hot. I don't feel like taking a shower. I have sweated in bed and I feel funky in my pits and groin. I feel the sweat—perspiration, a Harvard man would say—along the side of my body and along the inside of both arms so that my arms stick to my body when I press them against me. I feel myself funky. I feel like I am funky. As if funky. Through the door I see a bulldozer pushing down a section of the jungle where they are going to build the oil storage tanks. Past that I see treetops wavering and then falling, and I think of the barefooted Thais at the bases of the trees chopping away, clearing a site for the permanent quarters near the barbwire fence.

I take a still-damp towel and wipe my face. I wonder what it'll be like having a girl here who can speak English. I wonder what it'll be like getting to know Asia through her. I'll be glad to see Childress leave. I'm tired of laying down with women I can't talk to—a different one every night. I stare. Toward the end, before I left the States, I couldn't talk to my wife either, I think about that for a while.

My boots are scuffed. I look down at them and try to think about napalm because I want to think about dropping napalm. The floor of the tent is rough. I jam my feet into the hollowed-out innersole of my boots. Time for briefing. I stand and visualize myself standing naked in my boots. Then I slip dirty undershorts over my boots and pull them up. Then I slip on my flight fatigues. No one can see that I am flying with no socks on. If I get shot down over the mountains my feet will freeze. I never think about getting shot down.

I leave the tent.

Childress...

"Goin' home tomorrow," I sing. I sit on the side of my cot and dry between my toes. I look at my watch and laugh. I think about the great stretch of empty ocean that lays between here and America. I'll enjoy every minute of it. Won't have to fly. Sit back and let Pan Am fly *me*.

I slip on my socks and stand up to put on my boots. "Hey, hey, hey . . ."

Stacy...

The bench is hard against my haunches. The Air Force has enough money to put backs on the benches. They don't want people to get comfortable enough to sleep, I think. I'm not sleepy.

Captain Peterson is briefing. He briefs the primary targets. Weather is always bad over primary. We always go first alternate because the weather over primary won't be good for months. Peterson leans forward. His face is bathed in the fluorescent light from the podium lamp. I hate the briefing because I've heard it sixty to seventy times. Peterson's given it two hundred times, but he seems not to notice.

"One-quarter-mile visibility with thunder bumpers over primary," Peterson says.

I squirm on my bench. Childress stiffens against me after I rock into him. "We're not going primary," he whispers out of the side of his mouth.

"I know," I say.

"Tell Peterson, the ass."

"Let the bastard do his duty," I say. Peterson lives by rote. I watch his dumb lower jaw move. He has a long, reddish face that looks still redder in the fluorescent light. The red EXIT bulb is the only other light in the room.

I'm better-looking than Peterson. He has blond hair. Most girls would think he is better-looking because he has blond hair. Thai people like blond hair. I think he dyes his hair. I'm gonna look and see the next time I'm close to him.

He turns on the squawk box and the weatherman's voice booms into the darkened room. "Weather over primary: one-hundred-foot overcast, one-quarter-mile visibility with towering cumulus . . ." Peterson snaps on a little light above a weather chart. He moves his pointer robot-like across an area just north of Hanoi.

The weatherman's voice is so loud it is distorted. "Any questions?"

No one asks. Peterson comes back into the podium light. The weatherman gives the weather over alternate. Peterson does not point to this area near Pleiku, but I watch it. "Any questions?"

No one speaks. Peterson's head moves out of the light as he puts his pointer down. His wife probably makes him dye his hair. His stupid, little, tight-titted, faithful wife who probably wants blond children.

Childress rocks against me. "No anti-aircraft guns," he whispers.

"Is that what he said?"

"Sure, you know they ain't got any near Pleiku." Childress laughs. There's something that I don't really like about Childress, and it's not a color thing either because I like Ben; but deep down I don't think Ben likes white people.

He told Childress once, right in front of me, that the white race is a threat to human life on earth. They didn't look at me. "What're you going to do," Childress asks him, "sit around and whine about it?" They talked for a long time like that, like I wasn't even there.

Childress...

I say, "Red Dog 2 is ready for takeoff." I watch to see when Red Dog 1 releases brakes. His nosegear tire is a little flat on the runway. I begin to sweat almost as if I hadn't taken a shower. Heat from the sun and the jet engines of the planes—F-105's and tankers—that have taken off before us bounces up from the slab of concrete. Number 1 fires his after-burners, sending flames out in back of him. Smoke drifts across my windshield.

I feel almost guilty having an easy one for my last. But there's always a chance that some lucky son-of-a-bitch'll get me with ground-fire.

Red Dog 1 releases brakes. I release. We roll.

I break ground and climb fast to catch Red Dog 1 as he levels his wings to climb straight out. I can see Red Dog 3 closing on me from the left. Red Dog 4 is sliding into position beside him. Sunshine flashes off number 1's wings and he looks like a silver bullet in the empty blue sky.

My radio is garbled. If there's a Mig-warning I

won't hear it, but there're no Migs down where we're going. Only some lucky son-of-a-bitch on the ground has a chance of getting me. I nudge my throttles.

"Red Dog 1 changing frequencies," number 1 says.

"Red Dog 2, changing," I say.

"Three, changing," number 3 says.

"Four . . ."

After we change frequencies I hear better. We start eastward toward the Cambodian border. There's a light haze across the landscape. For a moment I almost wish I'd see a Mig today so I could get me one before I go home. Win another medal. Take it back to Baltimore and wave it in the Man's face.

When he says: "Boy . . ." I'll say, "Boy, my ass," and slap him across his motherfuckin' nose with one of my medals.

"Turning," Red Dog 1 says.

"Turning," I say, and tuck in close in the turn. I look down through the haze and try to locate the large lake north of Phnom Penh, but it is too far away and a little behind us. I strain to look back over my shoulder, then I turn around to keep number 1 in sight. The Mekong River is barely visible ahead of us. I watch it as it seems to slide in our direction until it is directly below us. I think: After today I'll never see the river again. We fly south where the river spreads out like a giant swamp. I rock my wings and look down.

"Turning," number 1 says.

"Turning."

"Turning."

"Turning."

The forward air-controller is southeast of us and we

take up a course to the southeast toward him. His radio is good.

I see him below us, flying slow just above the treetops. The trees lie like a hedge field beneath him, and he seems to hang blue-silver and motionless above the green hedges.

"Do you have enough fuel to work with me a half-hour?" he asks.

Red Dog 1 says, "We can stay for a half-hour."

"That should be enough. Do you have four birds?"

"Roger, four chicks," Red Dog 1 says.

Forward air-controller directs us south toward our target. Mare's-tail clouds lay between us and a flat narrow road which zigzags out of the mountains off to our right and runs straight toward the river before it disappears into a swamp.

We make a low pass to take a look, then pull up to wait for forward air-controller to drop a smoke marker where he wants us to hit. We come back across flying northeast and see bright orange smoke from the marker drifting up out of the forest.

Forward air-controller says some Gooks in trucks pulled off the road northeast of the smoke. We come back across flying southeast. The lush foliage is thick enough to hide something as large as a group of trucks. I try to spy the path that they made getting off the road, but the jungle has enveloped everything. We streak across too fast for me to see much, but I wonder if there is some lucky son-of-a-bitch down there in the trees waiting for me.

Red Dog 1 and I come in first. Number 1 lays his bomb close to the road. I come across. My stomach is knotted, tensed for the first burst of machine-gun fire. I put mine closer to the smoke and pull up too soon to see if we've

knocked anything loose. Three more bombs to go. No machine-gun fire, yet.

Number 1 and I climb and circle back while 3 and 4
come across.

I watch my instruments as I come down again, lower,
and I wait for some unseen hole in the treetops to begin
cracking with machine-gun fire. Red Dog 1 has hit on the
road. I oblique to him, pull level and let the hedge-green
trees shoot under me. Then all of a sudden I pitch up and
crash my bomb into the trees directly on the smoke. Then I
pull straight up, spinning. Not that time.

For a moment I feel giddy and I am aware of my hands
sweating on the stick. For some strange reason I want to see
the trucks. But then I think it would be stupid for me to get
shot down on my last one. I think about Ben and my moon-
faced, yellow-brown whore who I risked a court-martial to
take away from a stupid-assed white colonel . . .

I look at my toggle switches and my fuel gauge. Because she thought I was a confused and fucked-up black
motherfucker like Ben. But I wanted her pussy, not her
sympathy. "Soul-brudder, soul-brudder. I'm same-same
you," she used to say. She came with me and then she found
I didn't need her love. I just wanted her to be with me. The
finest whore south of Bangkok . . .

I come down almost to the top of the trees before I realize I've forgotten to flip my toggle switches. I tell Red Dog
1 my toggles are stuck. I break away from him and roll over
and come across upside down, screaming, then pull up just
enough to turn over and let my bomb fly into the orange
smoke, then pull up, spinning.

Ben might fall in love with the bitch. She would fall in

love with him. Ben might divorce his wife, with his silly-ass self, and marry her and take her back to the States and settle down near some nice liberal college and be happy for life. Pretty bitch. Soft. Loyal. Smooth-skinned. Ah . . .

We cloverleaf and come back across target for the last time and I think: If they don't get me now they never will. If the trees don't open up now and swallow me they never will.

Forward air-controller says, "Number 2, you're too low."

I go lower. Fuck him. I lean forward and look but cannot see, then I tilt to the side and let the last one go and convince myself that I hear metal crash against metal as it explodes, and I climb straight up, past number 1, and the pressure locks me to my seat. It is over. It is over. I laugh until I almost cry.

Ben....

For me this war is like Harvard. Nothing in it seems real. Everything is abstract. Everything is an argument or a question.

I should've joined the infantry, been splattered with blood, then it would've been real. This is like Harvard. The killers never see the killed.

Maum lights another reefer. When it's possible to kill without seeing blood, then it's possible to kill without remorse or guilt. "I've never seen a person die in this war," I say, but I know she does not speak English. She smiles. Then she frowns playfully because she does not like marijuana herself, but she never complains about lighting one for me. Oriental women never complain about anything, I think. I dry my right hand on a towel on the floor, and take the reefer from her and take a heavy drag. I hold my breath to allow the stuff to soak into my lungs. In the abstract situation I'm in, I can only hate whitey for the smaller symptoms of the disease that he is spreading around the world, like segregating the whorehouses and bathhouses over here.

Maum lifts my left leg out of the tub and soaps it. Like trying to get the Thai girls to hate Negroes by telling them niggers have tails and niggers have big dicks and will hurt them. Maum drops my leg back into the water. She walks around to the other side of the tub and picks my right leg out of the water and soaps it. She hums a little and smiles. I watch her soft, round, smooth, completely hairless, brown-yellow face, so inward-seeming as if she could teach me things that the narrow gnomish bastards at Harvard could never teach in a million years. If she could only speak my language, or I hers. I shiver for a moment, knowing that I don't want to go back to America with all this hatred in me.

I should never have come into the war but I came like a sheep. During all my life in America I've been led to loving the wrong things and hating the wrong things, like I was nothing more than a goddamn sheep.

I lean forward for Maum to soap my back. I keep on letting myself be led the wrong way because our survival depends on our lying to ourselves. Is that it? Maybe I really want the VC to win.

Maum soaps my chest. "Mass-sagee, mass-sagee," she says while helping me out of the tub onto the massage table. I lie on my stomach. She begins to knead my flesh like black bread dough. I keep my head hanging off the table so I can smoke my reefer. Blood runs to my head.

She has smooth legs and small feet. She pulls herself up on her toes as she kneads the flesh on my rib cage. I watch her little toes grabbing the floor. Then she gets on my back and walks around, breaking all the stiffness in my body. Her toes grab my back like they did the floor. I moan a little be-

cause it hurts and feels good at the same time. She snaps my
arms and legs, then she slides to the floor again while I turn
over on my back. She puts a towel over my erected penis. I
take the towel off. She blushes. I do not smile back at her.
She stops smiling. "Mass-sagee, mass-sagee," she says and
takes it in her small yellow hand. I shake my head No. Then
I pull her up on the table with me.

Childress...

The Blue Sky Bar is crowded and loud. My whore and I come into the main room, which looks like nothing so much as a long lean-to with a concrete floor and crepe-paper streamers hanging from the ceiling. A row of whores sits near the bar. A single light bulb illuminates them as they talk to each other. The jukebox, playing Aretha Franklin, glows in the dark near the door. It makes me think of a red-hot, pot-bellied stove. All the corners of the room are dark.

Another small light bulb hangs from a cord near the center of the dance floor. A few black GI's are dancing with whores.

Ben and some friends are sitting at a long table, talking shit. I sit down next to Ben. My whore sits across the table.

"Hey," I say.

My whore says, "Hi." She smiles, her teeth are perfect.

"Lieutenant Childress, Damg. What's happening?" Ben makes a slight bow toward both of us. "So you're finished?" he says to me.

"Yeah."

"I bet you glad."

"That'd be a damn good bet," I say. Ben slides his glass across the oilcloth table. I sip. Damg sips. "Scotch. Nice," I say. Ben signals for the waiter to bring two more glasses.

My whore listens to Ben's friends. Ben and I talk, but I listen to what my whore is listening to. A fat dark-skinned GI says, "That's how the Chucks got ahead of everybody else in the world. Because the average motherfucking Chuck doesn't feel anything. He acts like his emotions are dead. I told this white boy the other day, 'At least I have a heart. You don't have one. You've got ice water in your veins. You would kill your own father if the price was right and say you did it for the good of mankind.'"

Another smaller GI adds, "I really don't think the white man can feel a motherfuckin' thing either. He acts like he's numb until he gets scared. Then one of them come crying to me, 'You think they're coming back?' Talking about the VC. I said, 'Shut up, motherfucker.' We were up near the DMZ. I think the only time a Chuck cries is when he's scared."

"That's one thing: I don't mind crying when I'm sad or when I'm happy or when I'm fucking—if it's good—" one GI says. They laugh.

The GI continues, "A Chuck never stops thinking. He can't even fuck for thinking. He can't dance for thinking. Here he is walking down the street in Bangkok. The nigger is looking at the Thai women, finest women in the world. You hear me, in the world. And he thinks the Chuck is doing the same thing until all of a sudden Chuck says, 'When the war is over I'd like to buy up some of this cheap property and hold it until the price goes sky-high.' " They laugh. "Damn."

My whore says, "Chuck have no love."

Ben looks at my whore. The others keep talking. "Like most of the antiwar motherfuckers. They ain't really anti-war, they're anti-getting-killed-their-damn-selves. A few of them care. But the vast majority of them don't give a damn about these Vietnamese people."

Ben and my whore glance back and forth at each other. I could never live it down if Ben took my whore right from under my nose. He'd love that. Peaches & Herb are singing from the jukebox. Ben's legs are moving under the table. I'm afraid he's going to ask her to dance, and they'll get to talking that wet-eyed shit, and she'll choose to go to the bungalow with him instead of me. Since I'm leaving tomorrow anyway. The two of them are alike anyhow.

The slow song ends. I relax. The jukebox plays:

> I just want to testify
> That you sure look good to me.

I think about the money I have saved during my eleven months in Thailand. In the dim light the Thai girls look like little yella colored girls.

A group of GI's are dancing in a line.

> I just want to testify
> That you sure look good to me.

I want to join in, but I sit still. Every third beat they stomp and the line slides in the opposite direction. Slide. Slide. Stomp.

Two Thai girls are shoving a huge black sergeant, trying to make him lose the beat. He laughs whenever he

double-times and falls back in step. His forearms are like
giant smoked ham hocks. He double-times. Stomp. The girls
try to pull him off balance. He half-times. Stomp.

> I just want to testify
> That you sure look good to me.

He grins and looks at the ceiling, confident now that he
is so far into his thing that he can stay in step without looking at the feet ahead of him. Half-slide. Long-stride. Stomp.
"A-a-a-ah!" He wiggles his ass, spins and slides. Stomp. The
two girls continue pushing at him. I look around at the dirty
place, at the mismatched chairs and tables. I think about the
matched-up, cleaner, air-conditioned white whorehouses up
the row.

Ben is saying something about flying. I'm ready to
leave. A slow record starts. Ben asks my whore to dance. I
grab her hand. "We got to go," I say. "I hadn't planned to
stay this long."

"Okay." He smiles. He stands up and bows a little
toward each of us and smiles like an ass. I know what he is
thinking. Everyone says good-by. We leave.

I hold her hand. The night is cool. I stop a baht-bus.
The boy says, "One man, two baht."

I say, "One man, one baht."

"One man, two baht," he says.

My whore tells him something in Thai. He pouts and
accepts the two baht for the two of us.

The air is peaceful as we ride along. Night air blows
into the open sides of the baht-bus. The small boy hangs on
the rear running board and jumps down whenever the baht-
bus stops to pick up other passengers. Each time we have to

slide farther forward until we are sitting directly against the cab, Damg on one side and me on the other. The breeze is not so strong. I can lean down and look through the rear window into the cab, past the driver and out the front windshield. I decide to take Damg to the luxury hotel that the Americans have built up past the base.

Through the windshield I can see other baht-buses racing toward us down the narrow road between garish little whorehouses with neon signs. They look like all-night, three- or four-lane bowling alleys with tin or thatch roofs. The Hong Kong-made signs: red, blue and green, blinking FLYBOY, THAI HEAVEN, SWEET HOME, YELLOW ROSE, BOOM BOOM ROOM, HONEY BEE, DREAMLAND, THUNDERBIRD.

Farther up the road, where the Americans are tearing down a mountain to get dirt to build a runway on the sand, the air is full of dust. We are near the base. Three white GI's get off the baht-bus. Dump trucks clog the road. Jet engines whine like wounded animals in the Siamese night.

Ben...

The Blue Sky is almost empty. I walk to the rear and ask Papa-san to fix some fried rice for me. Then I walk over and sit on the concrete floor near the well. The other GI's have gone to the bungalows to sleep with their girls, or back to the air base. I don't want to sleep with anyone. My head hurts from too much scotch.

Papa-san watches me while he cooks, but I don't want to pretend that I am cheerful in order to prevent him from feeling sad that I am alone.

He cooks over a small blazing fire in a pan which he never sets down unless to add more ingredients. The food sizzles, and he lets the smoke come up into his face as the small flames lick up from a bed of rocks and touch the bottom of the pan. He serves the fried rice in a wooden bowl. I pay him a quarter. There are large reddish shrimp in the mixture but I don't feel like eating.

"Lieutenant?" he says, "Lieutenant?"

I smile.

He goes back to the fire, whispers something in the ear of his youngest son and sends the boy off on an errand. I hear the boy running barefoot on the stones outside the rear compound fence. The old man is plump. The faces of his family are lit by the light from the flames. They sit without eating, without talking; they are simply there.

The son returns with a thin, youngish girl. Her clothing is wet in spots, which makes it apparent that she's been working in a bathhouse. Papa-san pushes her toward me, saying, "You sleep with her tonight, Lieutenant."

She takes the last few steps toward me as if she has not lost the momentum from his push. She is a dainty, eighty- or ninety-pound girl with shoulder-length hair and a small mannish shirt covering her pointed teen-age breasts. She tucks her head and blushes. Her shorts are white like the shirt and she has a Scottish-plaid belt holding them up. She would look tinier yet if she didn't have high-heel shoes on over her white bobbysocks. She is amusingly beautiful. Papa-san and his family are happy that I have someone for the night.

"No, Papa-san," I say.

"She no have VD," he says. His voice quickens and rises to assure me. He shows me her card which has a blue circle on it to show that she has passed her last VD inspection. He takes my hand and places it to my ear. I know I am supposed to take wax out of my ear and rub it in her pussy to see if it burns her, but I do not. "I don't want to pom-pom," I say.

The family laughs at the way I say pom-pom. The youngest son urges me by slapping his hands together to make the sound that two bodies make slapping together.

The entire family has turned to look at me—four children, a wife and a mother. I hear a transistor radio playing from one of the bungalows.

The girl is embarrassed. "We walk," I say.

"Chi," she says, and the old toothless woman sitting on the other side of the flames shakes her head Yes.

"Beautiful, poo ying," I say.

We leave along the back path in front of the dark wooden bungalows where several GI's are sitting out with their girls.

The bungalows are in a row like a series of outhouses in back of an old Southern church. A wooden platform runs along in front of them and a naked shiny-skinned GI runs down the platform to where the vat of water is. He squats and washes his privates, then tiptoes back past us into his bungalow.

For a while the narrow path leads into the jungle before it turns toward the main road. The girl and I hold hands as we walk along the ditch that carries waste from the tapioca mill down to the ocean. The girl laughs and holds her nose at the wet-dog odor of the ditch. I laugh.

For a moment I wonder what would happen if I disappeared forever into the human and bamboo jungles of Asia.

We reach the road and walk along the stony shoulder. She takes off her highheels and walks in her socks for a while, then she takes them off too. In some places the air is chilly, and in others we walk through warm air. Walking through ghosts, we used to call it down South, before Harvard, before everything became literal and scientific, and then became more unreal than it ever was before, leading straight to Vietnam. Before a million explanations came down between me and what I want to feel, and then all the explanations proved to be lies.

As I walk I feel strangely free, and I dread the thought of going back to America. I don't know how I can ever feel right about America again, after what they got weak-assed me to do over here.

I want to go to graduate school, but I know I'll never sit in a class and learn from a white man. And who will I work for, and where will I go.

The road turns out of the trees and runs along the beach. The gulf is empty and the black morning is peppered with stars. The air on the beach is cool. I feel the presence of billions of people around me whose lives are menaced in the same way that mine is. Like the millions of Chinese who were slaves in their own country for centuries.

We walk down toward the water's edge. There is nothing man-made in sight except for a puny wooden dock where the trucks come down to pick up the ammunition and jet fuel from the ships anchored in deep water.

"Pom-pom?" the girl says in a weak voice and sits down and begins to undo her shorts.

"No," I say, and take out my wallet and give her five dollars anyway. Tomorrow I want to bring Damg on this same walk. We could sit on the edge of this continent which has been kept under the foot of white men until finally China had to get an H-bomb and say, "No more." And the people I am fighting, me, in Vietnam had to say, "You can kill me but you can't enslave me any more."

I look out across the water. Bangkok, Rangoon, Kuala Lumpur, Djakarta, Calcutta—dark music—and then across the Indian Ocean to Africa.

Stacy...

The water is cold. I try to turn hot water on but none comes. I get wet gradually and then I stop shivering as the cold water comes down across me. I look through the door down toward where they're building the new runway. Then I see Childress walking toward the showerhouse. He is almost a silhouette against the clear blue sky. I can see that he has civilian clothes on. He must be just getting back from town.

He walks slower than usual. But, I think, there is no reason for him to hurry since he doesn't have to fly this morning.

"Just back from town?" I ask.

"Wheew! Yeah. Walked all the way for a change." He sits down on the showerhouse stairs and takes off his shoes.

"Having your last big fling?"

"Yeah. I feel sweaty, funky and drunk." He stands up. "Tonight I'll be in Bangkok. Friday, Hawaii. Sunday, San Francisco. How about that shit?"

"Shit, I wish I was leaving too."

"It takes time, my boy." Naked, he walks up the stairs, turns on a shower and slides slowly under the water. I watch his toes curl up until he gets used to the cold water, then his feet relax and flatten out on the wooden floor.

"What about your whore?" I ask.

He laughs slightly. He takes water into his mouth and gargles briefly. He spits. "She's fine. Beautiful as ever with her Chinese-looking self."

"I mean about Ben," I say. "You said you wasn't going to let a Harvard-trained dude inherit the best whore in Thailand."

"I know," he says.

"But there's no way you can stop it from back in the United States, is there?"

The water seems to freshen his appearance. He spits again. There's something frightening about his naked, muscular cleanliness. I step out of the shower and stand on the steps drying myself.

"I hid some communistic papers in her room," he says.

"So?" I stop drying.

"Now all I got to do is call the Office of Special Investigation." He is out from under the water standing in the showerhouse door. "When they find the literature, they'll swear that she's a communist. See? And no red-blooded Amurrican, including Ben, will be allowed within a mile of her."

I look at him.

He steps out of the shower onto the top of the stairs.

I feel empty inside.

"It's as simple as that."

"I bet."

"Really," he says. "Ben doesn't need her anyway. He has a wife at home—named Rose, I think. Pretty little sister too." He laughs.

All I can think of to say is, "You didn't bring a towel to dry yourself."

"I can use yours when you get finished," he says. "I'm not afraid of catching white folk's germs."

WASHINGTON, D.C.

Rose...

I scoot the chair forward. It is rigid under me. Its steel legs scrape stiffly against the green marble floor. I see Calvin, in a yellow shirt, coming down the aisle. I let my eyes go out of focus. He is simply a blurred shape working his way along between the rows of IBM machines, with a smaller blurred shape, Edward, in a white shirt coming along behind him. I cannot see the cart, but they are separated by the length of the cart that he is pulling and Edward pushing. The cart itself is hidden behind the machines.

I pretend not to be watching, but watch. I watch with my eyes still out of focus, acting silly. I smile to myself, still focusing on nothing, seeing only watery shapes as I watch them picking up the cards from the other machines.

I put another card into my machine and watch as it rides smoothly across to the reading station. Then I focus and begin to punch the keys slowly. I hate this place, I think.

I look at the list of numbers. Then I punch out the last

number on the page. The machine hums. My bare knees are warm underneath. I turn the page and focus on the top number of the seventh page. The number is full of zeroes. I count them. Four. I punch slowly, 12-84-00003.

I hate this place, but I got to stay here for at least eight months until Ben gets home. I can't let myself quit this like I quit everything else. I got to stick to something.

My eyes go out of focus again. If I hadn't failed Ben I'd be free to sneak and give Calvin some ninnie, like I know I really want to do, instead of having to sit on it for eight months and wait to do right by Ben before letting myself do wrong with someone else. "That would be dirty, Calvin," I say to myself.

Ben needed another kind of woman, though. I was never comfortable with him.

I punch out the next number. The expression on my face begins to sour. Ben married me because he had to learn again what it means to be black after four years of Harvard. I should have helped him with that. But I was too busy wanting to be white, too busy trying to be like them. Here I was, somebody who had never known a white person personally in my life, suddenly given the chance to be around them, to have the things they had, to be married to an officer instead of to an enlisted man.

I wanted to be treated like their women are treated, not because I really wanted it but simply because their women were treated that way. So I wanted to be put on a pedestal too. I wanted Ben to do it.

Ben said I hated him because he wouldn't play husbandsy-wifesy games like the white people on television and on base do. I wanted to be the little woman, the modern

American housewife with the little apron and all. The great little housekeeper with the French Provincial furniture to dust every day while I waited for hubby. That's the goddamn truth, I think. Ben wouldn't cooperate so when he wanted me to be the first officer's wife in the Air Force to get an Afro I went to the beauty parlor and got it straightened as slick as they could make it, and dyed it red, like a fool.

But then, as soon as they took him to the 'Nam, what did I do bigger than shit but go right out and get the biggest, bushiest damn Afro you ever saw. I could do it after he was gone, but while he was here I couldn't have the thing sitting up there on my head, saying every day that he was right, and I was wrong. Oh no, I couldn't give him that. Shit. I feel like spitting in my own face.

Calvin...

There's no such thing, I think, as we come down the aisle picking up the IBM cards. I don't really give a fuck what they say. All you can have is something that hangs together for you. That's all. I slide my feet each time because I only get one step in as I move from one machine to the other. I pick up the cards on the left. Edward does the ones on the right.

Then I look up and think: She wants to pretend that she hasn't been looking at me. I saw her looking when I came off the elevator. Sooner or later it's got to happen—with her old man gone off to the war, too. I just want to be around when it do happen. She is small behind her machine, with her jet-black Afro teased up high on her head.

Of course she's gon' pretend that she doesn't want to talk to me either, but she's jive. She might be scared. She knows I can talk a hole in her drawers with her old man gone.

Edward pushes the cart tight against me. I keep my

hands behind me holding it away from me. Slow down, man, goddamn, I think, you must think these white people are paying you piecework.

I knew she was looking. My mind was off arguing something else, true, but you can tell when someone is looking at you—especially a bitch. So when I got off the elevator I started down the aisle cool enough with one shoulder low and a kink in the flow of my hips as I slid my foot along from one machine to the other. And I had my pants jacked up high so the "reaper" could ride my leg so she or any of the other bitches could see it if they were interested. Which they were. I laugh.

"Hey, it's me again," I say without looking at her. I pick up the cards from the machine ahead of hers. Then I look at her. She is punching keys. "Hey," I say.

She smiles and finishes out the number.

"Damn, you looking good. If I ever commit rape I want you to be my first victim."

"Oh, Calvin, you say the sweetest things." Her voice is full of sauce.

"Hey, one minute." I help little Edward get the cart turned around with his helpless Uncle-Tom self. He starts picking up the cards on both sides as he goes back up the aisle faster than the both of us came down. I turn around and try to hit on my man's wife.

Rose...

"Why don't you lemme take you to the party tonight?" he says.

I finger my wedding ring. Then I slide it up and down on my finger, like I am tempted to take it off.

"That's okay, I'm married too," he says. He leans on the machine.

"Calvin, you know I ain't goin' nowhere with you."

"Shit, don't say never."

"I didn't say never."

"Yeah, I noticed that. You used to say never." He mocks me, " 'I ain't never goin' nowhere with you.' Getting rough, ain't it, baby?"

I laugh.

He says something else. I watch his straight even teeth while he is talking. His features are round. His skin is very smooth and black, and he looks nice in his open-collared shirt. "You're letting them waste your life," he says.

I have to admit to myself that I've often wondered how

he'd be, but I've never wondered it before while he was standing up in my face, trying to look cute—and looking cute, in a way.

"You let 'em waste your life." His lips come down over his white even teeth.

I bite my lip and smile. He is an easy man to be with. Ben was hard to understand, but I can't blame it on Ben totally. I was confused too. I didn't give poor Ben a chance. I was too busy trying to be a socialite. I laugh about it now. He used to say, "All you wanna do is sit around the Officers' Club and sip tea with a bunch of empty-headed white bitches—with *the girls*," he used to say.

And I'd say, "Everybody didn't have a chance to go to Harvard like some of us."

"Now you know that's not what I'm talking about."

"Do you want me to stay around the house all day?"

"I just don't want you sitting around sipping tea and munching crumpets all day, with your long white gloves on and a little pillbox hat sitting on top of your fried head, grinning and saying shit like, 'oh, you don't say,' or 'how perfectly darling,' or 'oh, isn't that absolutely lover-ly.' Shit." He laughed and walked around the living room with his wrist limp, imitating a woman.

"You look like a faggot anyway, you don't have to pretend," I said. He should have gone up-side my head, but he didn't, and every week I was back over there sitting on the ball of my ass, which my girdle kept so tight that I forgot there was a hole in it.

Calvin keeps on talking. I could drive poor Calvin crazy like his wife already done. "Look, I ain't got that much time. Let me take you to the party?"

"See me before you go home," I say.

"I heard that before," he says, and continues talking.

I made Ben bring me long white gloves from Spain, and a wig from Formosa. The wig is right there now on the styrofoam dummy on the dresser, which shows that I ain't too sure of my Afro conversion or I would throw the thing away or sell it. I made him buy me a ball gown and take me to the Commander's New Year's Eve Ball, where he didn't want to go because the Commander hated black people. I forced him to wear his military formal, which he hated. And there we stood all night like two rigid smiling fools. I feel like spitting in my face, whenever I think about it.

Calvin says, "You see what I mean?"

"Yeah," I say.

"Shit, you don't see nothing. I don't want to keep it. I just want to use it for a while." He laughs. Then he looks at me like he knows something about me, but there is nothing to know unless he knew that Ben started running around about a month or so before he left. I hate for a man to look at me like that. His thick lips are pinched at the corners. He tilts his head to the side. He *is* cute. There's a lot of mahogany in his complexion. His eyes are very clear for a man who drinks a lot. I wonder if he thinks I'm going out with him just to get even with Ben. "You just need to get out more. Shit, I bet you dance like people were dancing when Ben— is that his name, Benjamin—left." He laughs. "Benjamin."

"That don't mean I have to go anywhere with you."

"If you go out by yourself crime-in-the-streets might get you, and since I know crime-in-the-streets personally, I gon' tell him to wait for you outside your house. Anyway, why waste taxi fare?"

"My husband left me a car."

"Excuse me." He laughs. "I know one thing he didn't leave you." He laughs again and claps his fool hands.

I look around to see if anyone is looking at us. "Why don't you do some work?"

"Why don't you let me take you to the thing?"

"Where?"

"You know damn well where. To the party."

"Oh, to the party." I act surprised. I want to get rid of him now.

"Yeah, to the goddamn party."

I laugh this time. "You're not getting mad, are you? Is Momma's little baby getting mad?" I stroke his long fingers hanging over the machine, then I pout playfully. "Yeah, Momma's little baby's steaming. I didn't want to hurt 'um's feelings. But 'um does look cute when 'um's feelings are hurt. 'Um's eyes get so pretty."

"Don't be simple, woman," he says.

"Aw, you know you got pretty eyes, nigger. Calvin, your eyelashes are naturally curly." I look close. "Unless you curl your eyelashes. You don't curl your eyelashes, do you, Calvin?" I laugh way back in my throat.

"Fuck you," he says, and rushes off.

Calvin...

Simple bitch, simple bitch, simple bitch. If I ever get her alone . . . I say to myself as I catch Edward. I bet I get her. I bet I get her.

Edward...

I see him coming and say to myself: Don't come rushing back up here after I done everything. I'm glad she turned you down. I hurry and get the cards from the last two machines. Hee-hee-hee-hee-hee. He can make the whole next round by himself while I sit in the basement and give myself a shoeshine.

Rose...

I get up and get more cards from the front desk. Then I come back and scoot my chair in under the machine. I hate this place. I watch the clock jump ahead. Then I punch out one number.

The day is hot outside, I remember. I almost wish I wasn't too lazy to go bike-riding. I could borrow Raymond's bike and Marcellus could ride with me. Friday. I've got the knit pants I can wear. We could ride out in Dupont Park. Calvin brags too much. If I was smart I'd find an older man who doesn't talk so much. I watch the clock. It doesn't look like it has jumped since I stopped watching it before. I might go to the party.

I stare straight ahead for a while. I'm sorry I hurt Calvin's feelings. But he does the same to me. I don't owe him anything. This morning he said, "You're looking uglier than usual for some reason today, Rose." And I like a little fool went into the ladies' room to look at myself in the mirror, and he was waiting when I came out. He said, "Girl, don't pay no attention to me. You were looking good."

And little Edward said, "Great God A-mighty," like he always does with his dirty little self whenever you walk past him with a tight skirt on.

And then Calvin said, "Can I take you to the party to-night?"

And I said, "I'm a married woman." And he said, "If you don't tell, I won't."

I watch the hands of the clock jump ahead. I'm certainly not going to give him any sympathy pussy. He used to score on me all the time. One day he told me, "You're almost the finest woman in D. C. except for one thing."

And I like a fool ask him, "What?"

And he laughed, leaned close to me and said, "Your hinnie is a little too big for your legs"; and he tucked his bottom lip in under his top teeth and stood there smiling.

And Edward sang:

> "Kildee legs and bony thighs
> Great big head and baboon eyes."

Calvin...

"The party is pretty good. I told you. Nobody here knows you or your husband. Quit peeping," I say.

"I ain't peeping. I'm glad no one lives in the basement or they'd have a headache by now," she says above the stomping and laughing and booming of the stereo. The speakers look like they're about fourteen inches apiece. Everyone begins to clap in rhythm and stomp like sanctified people in church.

"Just as well get us some too," I say, and start to dance. She joins the clapping. By the time the thing gets good the music is over. We lean back against the wall. The large room is crowded.

Nearly all night her mind has been somewhere else. Maybe she feels guilty, I think. I decide not to test it. I can see in her eyes that she is thinking about something else. I'm tired of talking to her. She dances nice and she looks good. Luscious. Music starts again. She moves nicely to the beat. I look around while we dance. Most of the girls here are from

Howard. I don't know too many of the guys. Maybe they're from Howard too, since they dance like they're from out of town—New York or Philly. Even if she hadn't come I could have done all right, I think. I look at my reflection in the window. I would have done all right, but I hate to mess with college girls. Too much confusion.

I look back at Rose. She has a nice little step. Small beads of sweat break out on her face again. I do the D. C. Bop. I lean back and dance wide-legged, swinging my arms like I have a big-apple hat in my hand. She smiles at me and starts into the little bit of the Bop that she has learned since coming to D. C. I fake to the right and spin her left. Then I fake left, spin her halfway right and jerk her back to the left. She keeps on around twice holding her arms in close to her body on the crowded dance floor. The guy should move the sofa, I think. Make everybody get up. We lean away from each other and wide-leg for a while. Then I drop her hand and we do the Philly Dog like the girl at work from Detroit does it.

Her small face is intense while she dances. The Momma don't play, I think. Her eyes are not focused on anything. It's getting worse, I think. I'd better take her on out before she tightens up. The music ends and we go back to the wall near the blue lamp. "I told you the thing would be nice," I say.

"Yeah."

"You don't want to say it but you know it."

"You got too many women, Calvin."

"I'm versatile."

"You better versatile on home to your wife."

"Aw-aw."

"I better go on home soon myself."

"Aw-aw."

"You can get messed up messing with someone else's husband."

"Shit, everybody's somebody's husband."

"You full of stuff, Calvin."

"No, I'm serious. Whatever don't already belong to somebody, you don't want. Hey, lemme talk to you for a while."

"Okay, I'm listening."

I frown. "Not here. Too loud. Let's dance one more time and fall over to my boy's house."

"Where?"

"Northeast."

"Calvin?"

"Shit, all I'm gon' do is talk. The options are yours. I ain't gon' touch you 'les you act like you want to be touched."

"The least you could do is get me a drink before we go."

"Okay."

I go to the kitchen. The kitchen is crowded with people eating ham and potato salad. I'm a little hungry too, but I don't want to take a chance on messing up so I hurry and get her a cup of wine punch. I dip my cup into the tub full of ice and red liquid. Someone pokes me in the ribs. I see that Rose has followed me. I guess she doesn't want to get too far from the decision she has made, poor thing. I laugh. We go back to the living room where the dancing is.

Rose...

The wine makes me think about it less. I feel funny too, as if everybody here knows that I'm married. I watch the Howard girls. Some of them have gone already. I feel much older than they are, though actually I'm not. Twenty. I should have gotten pregnant before Ben left. You can go crazy living in a house by yourself full of the things that remind you of how you and your man didn't get along. The furniture, my clothes, the wig, the green shoes, my leather purse—all remind me of battles we had.

I don't want to live in that place by myself. I should go home and stay with Momma and them.

I slow-dance with a stocky black man who smells like tobacco. His sports coat is wool. It hurts my face. His hair smells good. Maybe I can't have babies. We never used birth control. I hate to go home by myself.

Calvin is no good. I should date someone like the guy I'm dancing with. I could get away from him any time I wanted to. If I go with Calvin I'll be convicting myself of something. Ben always said I gravitated toward a clothes-wearing shit-talking nigger, rather than one who was trying to do something. Gravitate. Ben. I smile. "Just so the nigger can talk shit, you don't care," he used to say. I never loved Ben.

Even though I know about me I can't try to change me. I wonder how Calvin's sweat tastes. I like Ben. From far away, I like Ben. The music stops. Calvin has been dancing with a yellow somebody. He picks our wine cups up off the floor behind the lamp table. I drink. Then we go to the bedroom to get our coats. I've got to get the oil changed in the car, I think, as we sort through the coats laying across the bed. Ben said to change it in February and here it is April. All I do is get in and ride, like he said. I'd ride it until it falls down and then get out and leave it alongside the road. We come back into the living room.

With our coats flung back we finish the last dance. His thing bulges in his pants. I don't pull away from it. Tall as he is it hits me belly-high. The music stops. We go outside. I button my coat and we go down the stone stairway. Oh Lord, I think. His hand is warm against my back like he is leading me to slaughter. The place on my belly where I was dancing against his thing still itches. I know he thinks he got me, and he has, but I hate for him to know it.

We go down the walk. His hand is firm against me guiding me toward his car. If I could feel a moment of indecision in him I could regain control, but he is firm for a young dude. Resolute, Ben would say. He probably won't even try to talk for fear of giving me something to pick at. He'll just start kissing on me.

A tall guy comes up the walk toward us. There is something familiar about him. His face causes a small explosion in my mind.

"Yeah," he says, and stops.

Then I remember he is the guy from Baltimore who went to Thailand before Ben. He taps his finger on my shoulder several times while he struggles to remember. "Nellis Air Force Base. Nellis Air Force Base," he says. "You're my man's wife. Yeah. I'm James Childress. I just left your husband about five days ago. In Thailand."

"Yeah? How's Ben?" I say. "How's he doing?"

"I got back Thursday. Yesterday. I'll be damned. Ben is fine. I'll be damned."

"How is he doing? How did you find this place?"

"Accident. Let me stop lying. I been looking all over D.C. for you." He rubs his chin. I don't know whether he is joking or not. He laughs. "You look very good for a lady in waiting," he says.

We walk back toward the concrete front porch. He is not handsome but there is something rugged and forceful about him. "I got a lot to tell you about Thailand," he says.

"I'm listening," I say. "I want to hear how it is."

Calvin drops his hands to his sides. "Ain't this a motherfuckin' shame," he says.

THAILAND

Stacy...

The inside of the bungalow is dark and cool. Cooler than the jungle outside, darker than outside, and cooler. Dank almost. I've never been in one of these before. Eight months in Thailand and I've never been in one of these. Nervousness fills me, almost as if one of the girls had come here with me. Embarrassment, as if I had brought one of the whores back and she had undressed and gotten under the mosquito net and was waiting naked for me to do something. Because I don't want to, because it's not right, because it's better to wait until you get married. I grin.

I think about Roxanne. I feel almost as if she can see me, and so I have to say to myself and to her, "I came down to find the papers that Childress planted on this girl, find them and burn them to save Ben some trouble. That's all."

Get the papers and get out, I think. Get them and leave before Ben and the girl come back and catch me. Then I'd have to explain.

I go to the door and look out to make sure no one is

coming. The bald yard is still vacant in the white moonlight. The two old women are still sitting on the veranda across the compound. Light from a small fire glows on their faces. A cool breeze blows in the window, taking the dank smell of the room out of my nostrils. The breeze is not strong enough to make my hair move, but it makes my forehead itch where my hair almost blows up off the sweating skin, sweating from nervousness in the relative cool of the straw and bamboo bungalow. I turn around and begin to look for the papers. First, I thumb through the pages of a stack of aging American movie magazines. The papers are not here. I look again. Then I turn around. The floor boards are wide enough apart for me to see light from the low moon shining beneath the bungalow, halfway.

I lift the mattress and look underneath. Then I sit it down slowly and run my hands along the covers and back under the large pillows. I pull the wrinkles I have made out of the wash-tired dingy sheets.

I start to look through Damg's clothes hanging from a bamboo pole catty-corner across a corner of the room. Most of the things are made of silk. They feel sleazy between my hands. I run my hands from top to bottom, then back to the top again of each garment. Nothing.

I pick up the water vat. It is slippery between my fingers and the butt of my hand. Coated with algae inside where the fingers are. I hold it tight and look under it, then I set it down carefully in the same wet spot.

Ben spends night after night in this place. I shake my head. How? It smells like stale Thai food. I look under a white suitcase. Then in it. I wonder if Childress really planted anything on her. Maybe he simply told me he did, hoping that I would tell Ben and thereby frighten him at least enough to make him uncomfortable around her.

I go back to the doorway. There is a flashlight coming down the path toward the compound. The light goes along the ground for a moment. Then it swings high against the trees. I watch it. I wonder who it is. I look toward the back window for an escape route. I would have to tear the mosquito net down to get out. I can still hurry down the front ladder and disappear under the bungalow. I wait to see if the light is coming this way. I see the beam come into the compound. The light swings upward. I freeze.

I'd tell him the truth. I promised Childress I wouldn't, but if they catch me what else can I do? I wonder will he believe me. He probably thinks white people are just nosy, perverted, he might think, especially the ones who've been here eight months without going with one girl. Niggers think it's unnatural to go without pussy. He might think I'm on a panty raid, or something. As the light comes toward the doorway I duck back. I hear two people talking. They laugh. One of them is an American. The American voice is trying to say something in Thai. The Thai, the smaller one, laughs. They both laugh again and keep on past toward the next bungalow.

I start to breathe again. It's not Ben. The American is fatter than Ben. I watch them go up the stairs. I wonder what an American man is doing back in the jungle this time of night with a Thai boy. They go into the bungalow. The flashlight goes out and candlelight flickers through the holes in the wall. They laugh. I hate this place. I think about Roxanne's hard cool cleanliness with her clean hair blowing in the cold wind of a Rochester winter.

I turn around and decide to look for the papers once more. A picture of Childress smiles at me from the small shelf next to the bed. Next to it is a picture of Damg, and next to that is a picture of a large black Special Forces sergeant. Damg must be a nigger-lover, I think. A row of perfume bottles and cosmetic jars sit on the bamboo crossbeam that circles the head of the mattress. I sit down on the dank-smelling mattress. The papers are not here. Ben does not believe in virginity, I think. Two dollars and fifty cents to sleep with a girl all night. I couldn't lay down with a woman who's been with other men. It would be like the other men were there in bed with us, watching, comparing. I feel my face flush with embarrassment. I look back at the smiling picture of Childress. I wonder does he really hate Ben. Does he really want to get him in trouble. There is a picture of Ben smiling too. Above the shelf is a picture of John F. Kennedy clipped from a magazine, and above that three pictures of nude white girls, clipped from a girlie magazine. One of the girls is smiling back over her shoulder; her naked untanned ass is pointing like a gun toward the center of the room.

I get up and look out the window past the net. There are a million places that Childress could have hid the papers. And maybe there never were any papers. Childress always did think I was gullible. Where would he have gotten communist material on that short a notice anyway? I giggle.

Ben...

Damg and I laugh as we come down the road away from the Blue Sky. The dark, dusty road is filled with baht-buses taking GI's back to base, or down to where most of the whores stay in the tiny raised bungalows in the jungle where rice farmers used to live before the base was built.

Buses pull off the road to pick up passengers and spew dust into the headlight beams of the other buses racing past. Bars along the road are closing, and people come out and fill the dusty air with laughter and yelling.

"You number ten GI," Damg says to me. I stay a few steps ahead of her so she can't hit me. I laugh. She runs, trying to catch me. Then she stops and curses in Thai. The rocks along the shoulder of the road are hard for her to run on in high heels. Horns blow as buses jockey for position and clientele, and dart back and forth across the center line, narrowly avoiding head-on collisions. What makes the whole thing look stranger and more dangerous is that in Thailand traffic keeps to the left side of the road instead of

the right. Just when I expect a bus to dart one way it darts
the other, narrowly avoiding a crash.

I look back at Damg. Her ankle-length dress sparkles
when headlights shine on it. "Come on, you know you had a
good time. You were laughing just a minute ago," I say.

"I forget that you number ten butterfly," she spits.

"No, number one GI. My heart knows only you," I
sing.

"Number ten," she sings angrily. "If you love Lict more
than me I cut you throat."

"My heart is true," I sing. I fold my hands across my
heart and tilt my head to the side like a Siamese doll. She
takes the opportunity to try and catch me. I jump away
from her into the weeds beside the path. "I don't like Lict. I
love you," I sing.

"I hope snakes get you."

I jump out of the weeds in a hurry, screaming and high-
stepping. She swings at me as I go by.

"You danced with Lict four times," she says.

"No. Impossible."

"You dance with her five times. Her husband cut your
throat."

"You said four."

"Six." She runs at me again.

I cross the road and she follows. The narrow dusty path
on the other side is easier to walk on. Several couples are
laughing and joking ahead of us. We can barely see them in
the dark now that we are away from the road but not yet far
enough for moonlight to come through the clouds of dust
made by the buses.

Lict's husband allows her to go short-time, but he stays

in the Blue Sky to make sure that she does not get interested in any one man. I always stay away from her because he makes me nervous. If Lict goes short-time and stays too long he will come in the back looking for her to make sure she hasn't run off with one of the GI's.

She is beautifully built, a little larger than most of the Thai girls. She has a smooth firm body that makes you think she would be strong in bed. But I'd be too nervous all the time I was with her, thinking about her husband out there beside the jukebox checking his watch. "I ain't interested in that broad," I say.

"Then why you dance with her seven times?"

"She asked me to dance. She kept coming up, asking me to dance."

"I make you dance," Damg says, and runs at me.

"I not butterfly you," I say. Then I begin to think that she is really mad and not just pretending.

"You do," she sings. "I have much love for you but you have butterfly in your heart." We turn down a narrower path and come around some trees. The air is clear of dust here, and we can barely hear the horns blowing on the main road above us. Light from small fires on the verandas of several raised bungalows glows against the black outlines of the trees. I let Damg catch me, and after she pulls my ear a few times we hug going down the path.

She likes officers because she is a snob in her way. I swing my hips into her as we walk "unh, unh, unh, unh." Then I think about how her little toes curl up when she gets close to climax. Quiet. She is quiet in bed. You have to get used to it if you're used to sisters who moan and cry and call on Jesus when it gets good.

Damg starts to gossip about the other girls in the Blue Sky who have to go short-time with many men to make as much money as she makes with one man, who she takes as her teelac for a few months. She has had two teelacs before Childress, and all her men brought her food from the base and gave her enough money to help her brother through school in Thonburi.

Air in the jungle is cooler than along the road. The trees protect the earth during the day so there is always moisture during the night when the green canopy seems to open up for the stars.

"We go Bangkok Wednesday," I say.

"Chi," she says. "I show you, you buy silk suits twenty dollar," she says. "Handmade shoes. Everything cheap. I show you very much quality."

We come to a field of tall reedy grass where rice used to grow until the stream was diverted through the base. "You buy gold ring. Gold very pretty on doom-doom puchi," she says.

"You think doom-doom puchi love only clothes."

"It is true," she says. We walk along the edge of the field. The moon is visible off to the left and we can see couples moving toward the compounds on the other side. We walk under trees again. A small spirit house which is made like a little yellow pagoda sits on a pole in Damg's bald front yard. We climb the spindly stairs. I sit on the veranda and take off my shoes.

My mother lived most of her life in Georgia. She used to say that she could smell white people. When she'd come home from work she could tell if a white bill collector or insurance man had been in her house while she was gone. She would sniff, "s-s-s-f-f, s-s-s-f-f-f, what white people've been here?" she'd say. Ninety-nine percent of the time she was right. I don't trust myself as much, but I get the feeling that I smell white people as I come into Damg's place.

We sit on the side of the bed because there are no chairs. I sprinkle ganja onto the brown cigarette paper. I roll it. Then lick it and wet it all over so it will burn slowly.

I take the first draw and pass it to Damg.

Stacy...

I come out the briefing-room door into the pale early sunlight. The door slams behind me. Bordreau is on his way in. "Go back. Might as well go back to bed, nobody's flying today."

"Weather?"

"Yeah. You know that. Every time we get scheduled for the big ones the weather turns bad."

"Makes you think that God is on their side, old buddy," Bordreau says as we walk back to the crew bus. He waves the other pilots back onto the bus. "No flying. God put a two-thousand-foot cloud-ceiling over the target," he says. The other men turn around to get back on the bus. Lieutenant Colonel Milligan, stonefaced, continues getting off, pushing his way through the crowd. "Are you sure, Lieutenant Bordreau?" Milligan says brusquely as he passes us. He is a religious man and he doesn't like Bordreau's jokes about God.

"Driver, hold fast, let me check," he calls back to the bus driver.

"Dumb shit," Bordreau says under his breath. His narrow Cajun face still shows the print of the bed sheets. "Dumb shit thinks if he scares the weatherman he can change the weather." We get on the bus to wait for Milligan to come back.

"I guess he didn't believe you, Stacy," Bordreau says as he sits down beside me.

"You mean he didn't believe *you*."

"I didn't want to fly today, anyway." Bordreau stretches. His crow-black hair makes his face look paler than it is, but actually his hands are paler than mine, hairier, resting on the back of the seat in front of us. "Did anyone get off?"

"Yeah. The first twelve birds. Ben got off."

"Shit, they're flying his ass off."

"He's going to Bangkok for R&R Wednesday."

"But still he must be racking up a lot of flight time. I was ahead of him by twenty hours when we got here. Now I bet we're even."

I look out the window. There's something about Bordreau that I don't like either. Yet he is the easiest white guy in the outfit to talk to sometimes. I wonder why. I wonder why I can talk to him and Ben and Childress. Two niggers. Two niggers in the outfit and I choose to room with them. I look back at Bordreau. "Actually, I wish I was flying too," I say.

"Be my guest," he says.

"You just as well fly them now as later." I laugh.

"Bullshit." He leans close. "I met this Korean whore last night. I think I'm in love. Clean enough to eat. Belonged to an Army General until his wife got wind of it. I got her now. You ought to see her. Tall. Something worth sinking your dong into." He closes his eyes and swoons. "She and I've got some unfinished business."

I look out the window again. "I think I ought to go get a flight on a tanker for once."

"That's up to you. I think I'd rather get a flight on a Korean."

I get off the bus and get a maintenance truck to take me down to where the tankers are getting ready for takeoff. Actually Ben doesn't have it that much rougher than anyone else, I think.

I get an okay from the airdrome officer and then crawl up through the hatch in the belly of one of the giant aircraft.

I show the pilot my flight orders. He pulls his earphones up from his right ear. "The A.O. said he would add my name to the manifest," I scream above the roar of the engine. He shakes his head Okay. Then I strap myself into the jump seat between and slightly behind the two pilots.

This is the first time in a long while that I have flown on anything larger than a single-place aircraft. I think about Ben. I've always tried to be as fair as I can. I tried to keep him out of trouble.

I wonder what will happen to poor black Ben if Childress actually did plant the papers on the girl, and called the O.S.I. Communism is not a joke. Something like that is not a laughing matter.

The morning is bright now. The cockpit is hot, but not as hot as the cockpit of an F-105 where the sun can beat directly down on you, and not enough room for air to circulate. The two pilots are sweating as they throw switches and read checklist. I look behind me. The navigator is studying his maps, and the boom operator has gone to the rear of the aircraft to check out the long refueling boom. I hear him over interphone checking out the telescoping lever to make sure it will be ready when a fighter comes up behind us in midair needing fuel.

"Actuator reset, boom stowed. Coming forward," he says. I look back through the cargo compartment door and see him walking forward. The compartment is as long as a bowling alley. The plane starts to taxi. He walks wide-legged to keep his balance. When he gets forward he closes the door and straps himself into his seat. "Boom operator ready for takeoff," he says.

"Navigator ready."

"Copilot ready."

"Jump seat ready," I say.

"Pilot ready."

We turn slowly. The pilot pushes the throttle forward. We move forward. Then I hear the brakes screech. "Parking brakes set," the copilot says. He is tall and calm. Hook-nosed, in the right seat. The pilot is fat and nervous. Most of his weight has fallen to his midsection. His head is very tiny beneath a squashed-down baseball cap. The ends of his hair are sticking out like chicken feathers in the back. He pushes the throttles forward and the engines roar. The plane rocks like a crowing rooster. The brakes hold it still while the engines want to push it forward. It rocks. The pilot holds the four throttles forward with his pudgy hands sweating.

One of them releases brakes and we start down the runway. I look out the windshield as the grainy concrete of the runway streaks by under us. I look at the airspeed meter and look forward at the end of the runway, beyond which is the ocean. I wonder can we make takeoff speed. I look back at the airspeed meter and look forward at the end of the runway racing toward us. I feel the fifty thousand pounds of combustible jet fuel slouching around in the belly of the aircraft. I know there is another tanker on the runway directly behind us. The pilot jams the four throttles against the fire wall. The airspeed meter moves up slowly. Oh, shit, I think. The pilot pulls the control column back, but we do not climb. We start out across the water only a few feet above the surface. The heavy bastard begins to wallow. I pray that it does not lose altitude. For a moment it sounds like it is breaking in two. Then I realize that the gear doors are opening. The landing gears come up into the aircraft. Then the doors close. The plane starts to whistle. We start into a turn. The left wing goes down and I think: What if it strikes water and cartwheels us. Break up and burn. I hold my breath as the wing dips toward the surface of the water. I keep looking out the left window as the pilot increases the angle of bank, almost standing the plane on its side. We stay in the turn through about ninety degrees. Then we level out and the bird starts to climb. I look back. The boom operator jokingly wipes the nervous sweat from his brow. He laughs.

We start to climb, and he gets up and goes to the cargo compartment. In a moment he comes back. "Landing gears up and locked. Gear doors closed," he says over interphone.

"Roger," the aircraft commander says.

"Climb power set," the copilot says.

"Roger."

"Heading zero-one-zero," the navigator says.

"Roger, turning," the pilot says and alters course a few degrees. "Steady on zero-one-zero."

"Air-conditioning masterswitch."

"Set," the copilot says.

Cool air begins to come from the overhead ducts. I relax. I think of how stupid it would have been to get killed on this mission. I came on it only to avoid the conclusion that Ben was having to fly more often than the white officers in the outfit.

"Coffee?" the boom operator's voice intrudes over the interphone.

The pilot gives him the high sign. Sweat flows from under the edge of his baseball cap.

"Cream and no sugar," the copilot says. He is sweating too.

"Regular, boom," the navigator says.

The boom operator goes to the rear. I unstrap and follow him in case he needs help with the coffee. A flying airplane is hard to walk in. I walk wide-legged. "Damn, that was a hairy takeoff," I say.

"I can tell you one thing, these birds weren't made to operate in heat like this," he says as he gets paper coffee cups out of the dispenser attached to the bulkhead behind the control cabin.

"I thought we were going to scrape water there for a minute." I laugh.

"If we had you wouldn't be here to talk about it," he says. He leans close so I can hear him above the roar of the engines.

The empty gray floor is tilted backward as we climb. The boom operator sets four cups on the galley. He pours cream in three of them and sugar in two. Then he holds each under the faucet of the coffee container. The black scalding liquid squirts out into the cups. The plane bumps a little as we go through a cloud. Coffee spills on the boom operator's hand. "Shit," he says and licks the coffee off.

The compartment darkens for a moment while we go through a cloud. Soon the windows lighten up as the cloud gets gauzy at the edges. Then we are out in the clear again. A larger cloud comes between us and the sun, putting a shadow on the windows on one side.

The boom operator takes two cups of coffee forward. I carry the other two for him, careful not to let the hot stuff splash on my hands. I hand them to him. He gives one to the navigator and begins to drink one himself. "Have a cup," he says.

"Is it good?"

"No," he laughs.

"Okay, then I'll have a cup." We laugh. "I don't wanna get used to good coffee. There ain't no good coffee in Thailand. The best is at the N.C.O. Club and that tastes like battery acid."

The hot black liquid pours into my cup. I let it come half-full. Then I release the button and the faucet drips to a stop. I put a lot of cream in. The cream curdles.

"We're going to lose one, one of these days, and then they'll build the runway longer." He is a short man with a prune face. He wrinkles his lips together. His chin wrinkles and his head turns red when he laughs.

"I hope I'm not on it."

He laughs. "If you ever fly on another one, wait for a cool day." He leans close.

"They don't have cool days over here, do they?"

"You got that right. You in helicopters?"

"No, F-105's."

"Fighter jock?"

"Yeah, we got scrubbed this morning."

"Weather?"

"Yeah."

"How many more you got to go?" he says.

"Thirty-six."

"Not too bad, then you can go back and get a decent assignment for a change."

"Are you kidding? I'm getting out. I've had enough of this bull."

"You're not in for twenty, huh?"

"Hell, no."

"I don't blame you. If I didn't have fourteen years in I'd get out too. The Service ain't what it used to be."

"You got that right." I sip my coffee.

"I don't know." He shakes his head.

"I think we should either bomb the hell out of Hanoi or get out of the war altogether. You can't fight a war with one hand tied behind you. I hate to say it, but you've got to use the big stick. You got to show them that you mean business," I say.

"You got that right."

"Shit, sometimes it pisses me off. I mean the whole country is going to hell," I say, as I let some coffee stay in my mouth until it cools. Then I swallow it.

"And back in the States you can't even make a decent living any more, for one thing. With taxes sky-high, a man can't make a decent living. I swear it's just like socialism." He laughs. "I always say socialism is a mixture of laziness, free love and suicide." His face wrinkles like a prune. "Hell, look at Sweden."

"The same thing's happening in America. Look at the hippies. Anyone that takes drugs is committing slow suicide." I laugh.

"And the niggers on welfare." He laughs.

"Yeah," I say. I think about Ben. For a moment I am afraid that he might be here somewhere listening to me—but how?

"What they need to do is kick some of the bastards off welfare and let them starve for a while."

"Shit, I don't know what's going to happen."

"Just one big rat race. I'm away from my family fifty percent of the time."

"When the country goes to hell, I got my place picked out."

"Where?" He laughs as if he is asking in on a secret.

"Australia."

"I don't blame you, or Canada," he adds.

"Pretty soon Canada'll be as bad as the United States. Watch."

"Probably so."

"I want a place to raise a family. You can't bring up a family in the States any more," I say.

"You're right. I got two boys and I'm afraid to death. They say they got dope in all the schools in New York. I hope they keep it the hell out of Arkansas," he says. "Where're you from?"

"Rochester, New York, but that's a million miles from New York City, thank God."

"You got kids?"

"Not yet. I got the little girl all picked out, though." I take out a picture of Roxanne and hand it to him. I smile shyly.

He holds it by the edges and leans toward the window in the overwing hatch so he can see it clearly. "Freckles. Pretty. Looks like a real fine girl." He hands the picture back and shows me a picture of his two kids.

"Nice." I hand the picture back. "The Australian government'll help you buy a farm. I can buy a little truck. We can fix up a nice little place of our own. That's the kind of life I like. Shit," I say.

Ben...

The earth is beginning to heat, and the hot ground sends thunderstorms rushing up under us like bubbles exploding upward from the bottom of boiling water. We keep flying north past the end of the refueling area. Mad Lady 2 finishes refueling. I come in slowly. The boom is bouncing around in front of me. I stabilize in the observation position and move in slowly as the stormy weather tosses the tanker and me up and down. The nozzle of the boom shoots out and locks into my nose. "Taking fuel," the boom operator says.

"Roger," I say. Then I get bucked off the boom. I come in again. Trying to hang on is like a piglet trying to suckle a sow with St. Vitus's Dance. I fall off again. My armpits are dripping wet. I wish I had showered. I stabilize and come in again. Ahead of the tanker the weather looks rougher still. I bounce upward and duck to the side, barely missing getting struck across the nose with the boom. I drop back to the observation position again.

Major McCarthy says, "Three, can you hang on?"

I say, "Number 3, trying again." McCarthy knows that if I can't hang on timid Brewster never will. And if all four of us can't get fuel we'll have to go home.

The weather is getting worse. I come in slow. Deliberate. The boom bounces. I watch it, keeping my arms tense, cautious, so the thing won't hit me across the nose. I don't have the time to look down, but I know we're over the mountains. The telescoping lever shoots out and the nuzzle hits me in the receptacle.

"Contact," the boom operator says.

"Contact," I say.

"Taking fuel," he says.

"Most of it is going overboard," I say. Fuel spray hits the canopy and I am blinded. A thunder bumper hits me from underneath and I am jolted up toward the tail of the tanker.

"Break away," the boom operator yells. I break down and to the right.

"Almost got one," McCarthy says. "I'm a little nervous."

"Yeah."

"Check your sliding doors," he says.

My canopy has cleared of fuel spray; I look out at the sliding doors. "They look okay."

"We'd better find clear air, or take it home," he says.

"Roger." I fall back from the tanker. We fly north over Laos, looking for smooth air. Then we climb four thousand feet and find it smooth enough for me to come back in. Then number 4 gets on. My arms are tired as I pull back and relax.

I don't see any need in going up to the target area. I can see from here that the weather is worse the farther north you get, but the stupid regulations say you have to fly over the area to make sure that by some miracle there is not a break in the clouds directly over the bridge that we have been trying to hit for three days.

As we fly across the blanket of clouds, broken occasionally by jagged black rock, I think that if there was a miracle it would be in the other direction. The sky would be clear all the way up to target, and right over target would sit a bank of clouds that would prevent us seeing what we were aiming for.

I stay in close to number 1. The sky always seems more dangerous when you cannot see the ground. If there were a Mig down there radar would not see it until it popped up out of the clouds in good position to shoot one of us down. If the North Vietnamese launched a missile it would force us below the clouds, giving the ground gunners a clear altitude reference on us.

I look at my Doppler. We are near target. I watch McCarthy tip his wings and look down. I turn up on my left wing and look down as we circle back around. Somewhere beneath the white cottony blanket is the bridge on the main trail-line from North Vietnam to China. It is safe from us, as if providence itself were protecting it and the supplies coming across it. I smile.

Stacy...

I sit outside the tent in the dark with my feet propped up on the shipping crate that Childress painted with red insignia paint and used as a nightstand before he left. The air is cooler here than it is under the dusty canvas. Clearer, at least. Negroes leave a heavy odor in a room. I pause at that thought. Then I argue with my conscience. It's true, I say. You go into a room where a lot of them have been.

I can almost see Childress with all his cosmetics spread out on his little red nightstand. He is naked and is drying himself and singing:

If you sprinkle goofy dust around my bed
 You might wake up and find your own self dead.

"Hey, Ben," he might say, "come here and scratch my back." Ben would say, "Fuck you, man," and Childress would say, "Aw, come on, Ben, ouuw, oww, ahhh. Shit, Ben, come on, it itches." Then Ben would say "Okay," and get up and take his Afro comb and scratch it and say to me, "I don't want to get dirt under my fingernails."

I laugh. Most of the men are already asleep because of the early takeoff times in the morning, a few others are down on "the strip" chasing girls. Others are at the Officers' Club. I can almost see dice rolling out on the green felt tables. Slot machines churn loudly in the air full of stale laughter, stale beer, and whiskey in glasses with melted ice and cigarette ashes. I've always hated the Club at night.

I pick at my old mosquito bite. What does a mosquito do, sting or bite? Bite, I think. The heat irritated it and my flight suit rubbed against it in the cockpit today. I look at my arm in the dark, but cannot see the red welt I feel. I saw it when I was in the shower today. I squeeze the skin around it trying to make something come out. I enjoy the slight pain. Nothing comes out.

Our tent is half-empty with Childress gone. Through the screen I see the legs of the cots standing isolated on the wooden floor. Twelve thin poles in the dark. Childress' things took up half the room. His nightstand full of shaving cream, toothpaste, hair grease and God knows what else, looking as disorderly as if he had not gone through pilot's training, as if he had not been made to live in military neatness for twelve months of his life.

His tape recorder with stacks of jazz tapes was under the foot of his cot next to his row of handmade shoes. His towel hung down from the foot of the bed. His things did make the inside of the tent seem less naked and ghostly than it does now.

I scratch the mosquito bite on my arm. Ben and I are too much at war with each other to be sloppy around each other. We have not talked much since Childress left. I look down toward the ocean. The flight line looks like a lighted football field. With the banks of lights pointed downward, the sky above the flight line is as black as the sky over the open ocean beyond.

I should polish my boots, I think, but I cannot make myself move. Tomorrow will be my sixty-sixth mission. Thirty-four more to go. Two-thirds gone. Maybe three months if the weather gets better. I think about Roxanne. What is she doing? It is midday at home. April. She's at school. I smile. Ben doesn't believe in virginity, but if you go to bed with a girl who has been to bed with someone else it's like having that someone else there in bed with you. Roxanne was a freshman when I was a junior. Every Monday, Wednesday and Friday I used to watch her on campus. For months I would wait on the bench by the entrance to the quad. I would follow her at a safe distance over to Kilmer Hall where she had a nine-o'clock on Mondays, Wednesdays and Fridays. I never spoke to her. I didn't know her name. I would wait for her to disappear into Kilmer before I would go over to my own class at Founder's.

I told Lionel Mitchell about her and sometimes Lionel would follow her with me, laughing. She was the most beautiful girl I had ever seen.

I get up and go inside the tent. I assume that our takeoff time hasn't changed. I put the flowered shirt that I bought in Hawaii on a hanger so it won't wrinkle, but I put my Bermuda shorts in the dirty clothes' bag. I crawl into bed, thinking about Roxanne. All I really want is cleanness and niceness. I close my eyes and imagine that a cooling flow of clean water is coming out of a cool gray rock, flowing gently down over me laying in the grass.

Some people say it's healthy. They used to say if you do

it too much you'll go crazy. Then they used to say if you don't do it you'll go insane. I don't think anybody knows for sure. I hold my tongue out, catching the cool water from the rock. I want to get married as soon as I get back. I smile. Touching her with my dong would almost be a violation of the Pure Food and Drug Act. I giggle and squirm deeper into my bed, ready soon to go to sleep.

Ben...

I come across the wooden footbridge, feeling she doesn't love me. She never did. I think that not just because she won't write. There are other reasons. I put Stacy's two letters under my arm so the sweat from my hands won't soil them. I'm tired of arguing it over in my mind, I think. If she wanted to write, she would.

The sun is hot as I come down between the tents. It's no excuse for her to say, "I'm no good at putting my thoughts on paper." She could put a goddamn X on a perfumed piece of paper and mail that.

Stacy's girl is duty-proud. How could she want to write every day—sometimes twice a day? I walk past the scheduling bulletin board where, at night, bugs crash into the electric lights that you have to turn on to see if there are any last-minute changes in takeoff times.

I wanted a letter today especially, since tomorrow Damg and I are going off to Bangkok. The screen door to our tent slams behind me. I throw Stacy's letters on his cot and lay down. He'll be back from flying in about an hour, I think. I kick off my shoes. He'll come into the tent and ask, "How'd I do?"

I'll have to say, "Two, Stacy. On your bed." His face will redden and flatten out when he grins. He'll smell the letters and giggle. As innocent of ill will as he is of insight— a big, handsome-in-a-way white boy. He might unzip his flight fatigues and rub the letters in his crotch and make a noise like he is masturbating.

I look at the picture of his girl taped to the front of his locker. I stare at it for a long time. Then I think about the picture of my wife taped to the inside of my locker. Hidden.

What does a woman see when she looks at him. A poor dancer, a stiff human being, someone ill-at-ease with women, a shallow person, a virgin. His handsomeness is rather ordinary. His face is like the face you might see on local television in Boise, Idaho, or Bemidji, Minnesota.

But being white, even people who don't admire him admire him. Even the people whose ass he kicks smile in his face.

I don't know if I envy him for being able to kill without remorse three thousand miles from home—kill simply on the chance that that killing might make the world a little safer for him and his. But I don't see why I'm helping him either.

I turn over when I hear the cleaning girl coming. The door slams. Another girl goes past the tent. I see her legs in bobbysocks through the screen. She drags her sandals in the dust. "Sawadee," I say.

"Sawadee," our girl says. She is short with a round face. She smiles. I consider leaving the tent to be out of her way, but I don't really want to stand out in the sun. I don't want to go to the Officers' Club. I haven't been to the library in weeks. Reading seems useless to me now. She picks up Stacy's dirty clothes and folds them for washing. She has hemmed the bottom of her skirt to make it a mini. "American girl," I say and point to it.

She hides her face, pretending to be shy.

"Your husband like?"

"Chi." She moves around to the other side of Stacy's cot. She makes the cot up, then places the letters back on top. I look at them. She sweeps the sand off the mattress where Childress slept. Then she starts the game that she has played every time I've seen her since Childress left. "He go back to U. S. of A."

"Chi," I say.

"He come back Thailand?"

"No."

"Oh." Again she sounds surprised and slightly disappointed. "Thailand love him very much. He same as Thai people, but big, big." She laughs. All of the cleanup girls liked Childress better than any of us. He joked with them a lot. When he found that most Thai people have never tasted apples, he ordered a bushel of apples from the commissary in Japan and passed them out among the girls. He knew how to jive them and he knew how to make them laugh.

They loved to laugh. Negroes used to love to laugh, I think. Is that a myth? No, I think it's true. I don't laugh much. I watch her fluff up the pillow. Her face is pleasant. Everything my wife did was an ordeal. She never stopped frowning from the time she got up in the morning until she went to bed at night. That's not completely true, Ben, I say to myself. I wonder why that is the only thing I remember about her. I'm a fucking abstraction. I watch the cleanup girl finish cleaning. I don't even know her name. Childress knew all their names. He taught them how to dance.

She starts out the door. "Koop kun," I say, barely remembering that that means thank-you.

"Koop kun mai," she corrects. She waits for me to say something else. I would like to joke and talk to her, but I always hesitate because I don't know what these people think of me. I have gotten into a habit of hiding myself. I don't trust friendliness. Harvard started me to believing that a smile covers malevolence as often as it does . . . malevolence, damn. Ben, you're a pitiful poor nigger.

I look up. While I was in my quandary the cleaning lady slipped out the door.

Stacy...

Bordreau and I jog up from the beach. By the time we get to his tent we are sweating. His roommates are gone, so I go in and talk with him for a while. Then I walk across to my own tent, thinking that it wasn't much use going swimming if you end up as hot as you were before you went. But I really like to stay in shape, so I guess the jogging did us some good. I blow out a deep breath as I come into the tent. "Hot," I say.

Ben is there laying on the bed, sweating slightly. "Takes your strength away," he says.

"Lucky you got any, you stay in bed so much."

"I'm saving myself."

"That's right. You're a night man. Hey, cat, why don't you go swimming with us sometime." I wonder if he's ashamed of the fact that he can't swim. Childress told me he couldn't. "We got an inner tube that can fit you."

He laughs. "I might. The sun's too hot."

"You need a suntan," I say, and laugh.

"I don't have to swim, all I have to do is lay out on the beach then." He laughs. "You're doing pretty good."

I put my arm next to his. "I'm getting there. Did you see the Colonel?"

"Yeah." He stands up. I sit down and wipe myself with a towel.

"What was it all about?"

"I don't know. They claim they're doing an equipment check, but they're really trying to determine if I was lying."

"When?" I wipe my hair.

"When I came back with a full load of bombs. You know, last week. I told you they wouldn't toggle and they wouldn't jettison."

"They didn't believe you?"

"I guess not."

I look at him. He begins to pace. I didn't believe him either. "They think you just didn't want to drop them."

"They're right, Stacy. I didn't see any troop concentration. It looked like a village to me and all I could imagine was millions of pellets of steel ricocheting through an un-bunker village. I couldn't drop them." He stops walking.

"Damn. Ben, you can't really tell what's a village and what's not, flying at six-hundred per."

"It was a village. I couldn't make myself drop them. I lied and said they wouldn't toggle."

"Damn, Ben, they're going to find out and fry your ass."

"Stacy, I decided what I'm going to do. When I get back from Bangkok I'm not going to fly any more."

"Why?"

"I'm tired of helping white men keep their hold over the world."

I look at him and want to say a lot of things but don't. "So that's what's been eating you ever since you got here."

He looks at me for a longer time than he ever has.

"Ben, they're not going to let you do that."

He does not say anything.

"Aw, shit, Ben. They're not going to let you stop flying."

"There's nothing you can do about it."

"You? You? What do you mean *you*? I don't give a damn one way or another. Shit, you can fly upside down and backwards for all I care." I get up and go out the door. The bright sun blinds me for a moment. I walk briskly away toward the Service Club.

Fuck you, Ben, I think. All I want to be is away from here. My mind begins to whirl. I think about Roxanne. I wish I could see her. Just get away from this place.

SCHENECTADY
FALLS, N.Y.

Lionel...

Roxanne and I get there late and come into the large auditorium that is dark except for the stage. I say, "Excuse me, excuse me, excuse me" as we side-step down the narrow aisle to where two vacant seats are.

I look at the stage. The last speaker is up. The speaker is a short red-faced man with blond hair, standing near the right side of the stage. I can tell that his speech is almost over. We bend forward a little and keep whispering, "Excuse me," as we go past turned-aside knees down to the seats.

I sit down. Roxanne sits and starts to take off her sweater. The smell of outdoors comes off. I help her get her arm out of the sleeve. The pink wool is soft. She folds the sweater and lays it across her lap. Her face picks up light from the stage in the dark. The blond speaker is saying, "Two excellent examples of this . . ."

People applaud. He pauses, then continues. "Two very excellent examples of this in recent years . . ." Roxanne starts to look around. I knew yesterday that she wouldn't be interested in this. She never pays attention to anything unless someone is talking about her. I watch her out of the corner of my eye.

If you could only find out one thing that she's interested in, I think. If she even knew herself . . . but she probably wouldn't tell even if she knew. "Oh, nothing," she'd say if you asked her what was on her mind.

She begins to read the program. If everybody else were reading the program, she'd be listening to the speeches. I hurt a little inside. I would like to be able to reach inside her and change that one little thing that keeps her from being a perfect girl.

The folding chairs are hard. She drops the program. I pick it up. She does not say, Thank you, Lionel, or anything. She thinks that people are put on earth simply to serve her. Ingrown.

She doesn't listen to you when you're talking, but she always wants you to listen to her. She's good-looking and so you do things for her, hoping that she'll at least acknowledge that you exist as a person.

She's not in love with Stacy. The speaker scratches his head. He's not much older than I am, yet he's the leader of the New Conservative Coalition, NCC, I think. He says, ". . . and that will insure a Republican victory in 1968, and thus . . ." People applaud. "And thus insure a return to the values that made America the greatest nation on this earth, bar none." We applaud. Roxanne claps her hands, but I would bet a million dollars that she doesn't know a word he said.

Roxanne...

I would rather be married in a house of my own than just sitting here waiting, I think. The auditorium is cool. I put my feet on the rung of the chair. The heels of my shoes kept my feet from sliding off. I sit still for a moment, listening. Then I put my feet flat on the floor and begin looking around again.

I wish I had gone ahead and married Stacy. I wish Stacy hadn't joined the Air Force. He didn't have to go. Janet's father could have gotten him out of it. He could have joined the National Guard for a few years and that's all there'd be to that, instead of running off to the other side of the world, for God's sake. Sometimes he makes me sick, always talking about his duty, "My duty." I see him filling his chest with air. What about me, Stacy, what am I supposed to do while you run all over the earth carrying the white man's burden?

I scratch my palms. I can feel the backs of both my hands. That is, I do not reach and feel them, but instead I just sense them, that is, the skin on them, and the skin on my arms. Cold. And on my thin ribs where the skin is cold also.

My thighs sit evenly on the unpadded folding chair, which would make marks across the back of my legs if I had not worn a skirt long enough to smooth down between the chair and the back of my thighs.

I sit forward. The skirt is actually not all that long. I think that legs look bad with big old red lines across them. Anyway, sitting forward will make people think I am really interested in the little speaker. He looks young behind the podium. Three other people are on stage with him. The woman is ugly. Big. Butchy.

I don't mind having small breasts. There's an advantage to it. They make you look streamlined and interesting in a wolvine kind of way. People notice you more. Marriage is better than being with Lionel. Ba-a-a-a-h.

I turn slightly and look at him and catch, out of the corner of my eye, a Negro sitting in the row behind us. What in the world is *he* doing here? I look back, pretending to look at the bleachers in the rear of the room. The Negro is tall, with hair teased up on his head and long legs in checkerboard pants curled up against the seat in front of him. He is two seats from directly in back of me. And lo and behold, right behind me is another darkie with granny glasses sitting on the end of his nose. I pull up on my feet and look above their heads. God knows I wouldn't want them to think I am looking at them. The one behind me stares right over the top of the granny glasses into my face. I smile. I turn back around and wonder what they are doing at a New Conservative Coalition meeting.

They couldn't possibly think that I was looking at them. I wonder if I should turn around again and look up at the bleachers so they will think for sure that I'm looking at someone. I stand halfway up and look along the bleachers to the right. Lionel, the dummy, asks, "Who are you looking for?"

I whisper, "Someone. You don't know them." I sit down. The darkies make me nervous. I hear them whisper something and I hold my breath, trying to make out what it is. The one right behind me laughs and they lean apart. The chairs on both sides of them were vacant so they are taking up six seats right in the middle of an auditorium where they don't belong anyway. That's the kind of thing that makes you mad. I burn hot with embarrassment. What would have happened if Lionel and I had sat in the two seats between them.

I feel nervous. The darkie behind me must be undressing me with his eyes. I turn slightly to the left so I can see the other one out of the corner of my eyes. He is looking right at the side of my face. I turn full-forward and try to concentrate on the speaker. He says, "As government grows, the concept of individualism declines."

I lean over to Lionel. "He's a good speaker," I say.

Lionel wrinkles his nose, signaling that he doesn't agree. I look frontward again. Lionel's nose wrinkling was stupid-looking. The image stays on my mind. Sometimes Lionel can make you sick. I wonder if that Negro is still looking at me. If he is and I turn around he'll be staring right in my face. I let my hair fall between him and the side of my face. I know at least that he can't see my eye, since when I look out of the far corner of my eye I can see nothing but my hair. Sometimes they act so biggidy. Maybe he can see my nose, but the only way I could know for sure would be to have an eye on the end of my nose. If that eye could see him then he can see my nose now.

You never know what they're thinking. You live on the same continent with them and you never know what they're thinking. Nervousness makes me warm all over.

Lionel...

"The burden is on us to safeguard civilization from the Mongolian hordes. If the Pacific Ocean is to become a Red Sea, then we must not allow it to be come Communist-red, but red with the blood of those tyrants who would seek to limit the American presence, who would seek to undermine American interest, who would seek to humiliate and frustrate the efforts of the Free World's greatest military power in this remote corner of the earth." The speaker steps back from the podium and sucks his teeth.

"The cost of civilization is always high, but brave men have always been willing to pay it, because the alternative is eternal darkness. If the proud white race falls there will be no later white race. There is no way to purify the blood once it has been tainted either with alien ideology or defeat," the speaker says.

Behind me I hear someone say, "I told you these motherfuckers are crazy." I look around and see two black boys sitting behind us. I wonder what in hell are they doing here and how long have they been sitting there. I turn back around after one of them stares me right in the eyes.

"Sh-h-h-h, I want to hear what this motherfucker's got to say," the other one says.

I look over to see if Roxanne has heard their profanity. She seems to be absorbed with some deep thoughts.

"I think these motherfuckers would rather blow Vietnam up than give it back to the Vietnamese."

"Sh-h-h-h," the other one says again.

The speaker is saying, "This is not a remote war, in a remote part of the earth, for if we do not stop them there we'll be fighting them in Los Angeles and Sacramento. We'll be fighting them coming across the Rockies. America does not seek empire. We have never wished to expand beyond the borders of this nation, but we must insist that no one encroach upon the land which our forefathers hallowed with their blood. We must insist that the only acceptable price for a share of the bounty that we have wrested from the unyielding hands of nature—we must insist that the people of Africa, Asia and Latin America become equal partners in our great struggle to subdue raw nature, and eventually bring the stars and moon into the service of mankind.

"In closing, I would like to say that America will be born again. America will be well again. America will remain the hope of the Free World."

Roxanne...

We come into the green hallway and push through the crowd of young people talking and laughing near the doorway. Cheerful. I smile and put my dark glasses on so I'll have both hands free to slip my sweater on. The hallway is cooler than the auditorium. I look around. The green tile ceiling seems very low. The ceiling in the auditorium was four times higher, with long fluorescent lights burning way up among the steel beams. I can touch this ceiling by standing on tiptoes. I wonder if the chair has left a red mark across the back of my thighs.

I turn around and see the two Negroes standing over near the water cooler, joking.

"I'd love to have a steak and a good hot baked potato," Lionel says. "Piles of butter and sour cream."

"Don't you ever think about anything other than eating?" I say. I wonder what the Negroes are laughing at.

"I'm hungry. I haven't eaten all day. What do you mean?"

"I haven't either, Lionel, but . . ." I start to move toward the side of the hallway where the Negroes are.

"Shit," one of them says. He laughs, buckles his knees and does a vulgar little wiggle.

"Damn, but all these motherfuckers might turn on us."

"Naw, man, how would that sound on TV: 'Two Negroes were beaten to death last night at an upstate Young Republican meeting.' " They both laugh. "Wait till you see these bitches. I bet you might say it's worth a little light ass-kicking to get into some of this," the tall one says. His hair is teased up about three inches, making him about six foot five from the top of his hair to his shiny patent-leather boots. About two-thirds of his height is legs, clad in blue-and-white checkerboard pants.

"We'll see," the other one says. He is wearing a green pullover sweater. "Maybe we shouldn't lay down with the oppressor. Maybe fucking white women is counter-revolutionary," the shorter one says. His granny glasses are perched ridiculously on the end of his nose. He looks out mockingly over the top of them at the people who he knows are listening to him.

I cringe a little at the language they are using, but I like the sound of the shorter one's voice. The taller one is better-looking.

"We've got a long trip back," Lionel says, "maybe we'd better grab a quick something to eat."

I pretend not to hear him.

"That's what I was saying," the tall one whispers urgently. "The average white man feels the shit. First his Chinamen started acting up on him, then his Vietnamese, then his niggers, and now his women." They hoot.

"Your wife gon' act up on *you* if she finds out we're up here."

"I feel sorry for him myself," the tall one says mockingly.

"I don't. I sent a ten-dollar contribution to the Black Panthers, the Viet Cong and Women's Lib, and I'd send one to the Chinese if I knew where to mail it." They laugh again. The tall one buckles his knees again and wiggles.

"You better quit talking so loud."

"It really doesn't matter that much to me. These motherfuckers might not fight, but they sure do control the police. Come in here with tear gas, billy clubs, dogs, mace, firehoses and shit."

"Fuck 'em."

"What we gon' do?"

"Shit, do like the Zulus did the British, fight them motherfuckers with sticks." They hoot.

Lionel takes my hand. He is listening too. "We might as well get started," Lionel says.

"Okay."

"Vulgar," he says as we move toward the door. Then everyone is quiet. I look around. Two white girls come out of the ladies' room and approach the two Negroes. The girls are laughing like women do when they have something planned. "Sorry to keep you waiting," the shorter blonde one says. She marches up to the tall Negro. The other girl is prettier. I am prettier than she is, I think. Her legs are a little heavier, but she's pretty, about eighteen years old.

"Whatever ya'll got planned, it ain't gon' work," the short Negro says. People part to let them move toward the door. The prettier girl is nervous like I would be. I watch them. I almost wish I were going with them, just to see what will happen next.

THAILAND

Ben...

The three of us drive to the marketplace to buy fruit to eat on the way. The driver gets out first and walks ahead of us and I move along behind Damg through the noisy crowd. I am happy to be away from the base for five days. I know what the Air Force will try to do to me when I insist that I am not going to fly anymore. I think about prison as we push through the noisy crowd of Thai people.

Food carts are jammed close together. There is barely room to pass. Damg is careful not to brush against anything that might soil her white cotton slacks. People watch us. I smile back at them. We pass the food carts and walk back past a group of food stalls and glass cases full of cooked rice, candied fish, edible seeds, dried squid, red Oriental sausages and a lot of other food I have never seen before. I wonder have the people in this small town, ninety miles from the base, ever seen a Negro before. The flies and noise swirl around us. Flies light on the food, but no one rushes to shoo them away. An old woman fans leisurely above a tray of sweets. I am no longer anxious about what the Thai people might think of Negroes. They smile and Damg seems proud of me. She struts ahead.

We walk into the shadow of a large building with an outdoor restaurant on top, where several rich-looking Orientals in sunglasses sit drinking in the shade of a giant parasol and look out past potted palms at the crowd below.

We move to the left toward an open shed which runs back to the canal. Inside the shed, plucked fowl and skinned game hang from wires in the dim light. Oranges, melons, breadfruits and mangoes are stacked in high pyramids on the ground. Damg and the driver pick out some good melons. She thumps them to see if they are ripe. We have attracted a crowd. I watch small fish wiggling on a bed of wet banana leaves in a box beside the pile of mangoes. A small boy picks up one of the wiggling fish in his hand and shows it to me.

An old woman whose teeth are red from chewing betel nut smiles. She laughs when I pretend to swallow the fish. I can feel all tension draining out of me. Thailand, I think.

"You like mangoes more than melons," Damg says.

"Either," I say. I give the boy back his fish. He drops it in the box with the others. Damg puts two mangoes in the straw bag that the taxi driver is holding over his arm. Then she drops three oranges in. She is always serious when she is shopping. Practical. I feel closer to her now than I ever have since I have cut myself off from everyone at the base. I wonder what Stacy is thinking. I can picture him fretting. He is a worrier. I like him okay, but I know he will never understand how I feel. We walk back toward the taxi. Not him.

As we drive, the wind is like a hot rag fanning back into

our faces. Damg and I sit in the back seat, eating. I turn toward the inside of the taxi to keep the hot wind out of my face. We finish the fruit before we get to the point where the road runs along the ocean. The air is cooler here. Between the road and the water is a row of bungalows sitting in tree-shaded compounds. Some of them are little more than Oriental pavilions perched a few feet above the clean tidal sand.

The taxi driver stops so we can watch a group of children giving whiskey to a brown bear. A boy takes the bottle down from the bear's mouth. Then the children sing and clap their hands and the bear dances. He turns around in a circle. The children are half his size. The boy puts the bottle back to his mouth again.

Damg gets out and feeds the bear the skin from an orange. He spits it out. She is beautiful running back to the car pretending to be afraid.

The beach road is shaded most of the way. Thai servant girls in green silk uniforms sit in the shade in front of some of the larger compounds. We stop at the far end of the beach to buy shrimps from a vendor. We sit in the sand and eat. A water-skier falls, gets up, and falls again. Far out, the sails of small boats sit almost motionless on water with waves no bigger than the waves on a Negro's head after he takes a stocking cap off. As I look out across the water, I begin to wonder what my wife is doing.

I look at the sky and think about prison. Being in prison must be like being dead. I lay back and close my eyes so that Damg and the driver will not notice anything wrong. The sand is warm against my hands, which I spread under my head, fingers laced.

I feel weak. They can do anything they want to me. They can put me in prison, and there's nothing I can do. They have no right judging me, I think. Only green men from Mars could give me a fair verdict.

Maybe I should never have come into the war. A Harvard man doesn't have to come into the war. There are ways of getting out of it. But how, I wonder, could I have escaped the fate of the oppressed without using the privileges of the oppressor?

Damg's shadow is over me. I feel her looking down at me. I lay still, as if I am asleep, but I know that she can see the tension in my face. I try to relax slowly. I unclench my teeth slowly. I let my arms rest fully on the sand. She moves and the sun hits my face again. Then her shadow comes across me from the other side. I wonder if the driver is looking at me too. I want to know too if there are the beginnings of tears in the corners of my eyes.

I shake my head and stretch, pretending that I am just waking up. Damg is smiling.

"We go Bangkok tomorrow. We stay Pattaya tonight so baby-san can sleep," she laughs.

"No," I say. The driver has spread the shrimp out on a straw mat. He pushes the mat toward me. I take one of the big shrimps and put it into my mouth. The warm meat mashes, then breaks between my teeth. The meat is plump and succulent, like lobster or king crab. I sit up. "No, I gotta get to Bangkok. Tonight. Tonight," I pant with my tongue hanging out.

"Mock-mock poo ying in Bangkok," the driver says, and does a wolf whistle. We both look at Damg and laugh. Then we eat the other shrimp and go back to the car.

After less than a hundred yards the road turns away from the beach. I look out the window. Three small girls are fishing in the canal. They lower a wicker basket into the swampy water as we approach. We come alongside them. They pull the basket up full of grass and mud. I look back through the rear window and see no fish in the basket. They fade out of sight behind us. Ahead a small boy sits astride a water buffalo while the animal drinks from the canal. The rice paddies behind the canal are flat for miles. The sun is already low and the rice harvesters, who usually stop working during the heat of the day, are back gathering the large bundles of rice plants, tying them and leaving them along the rows as they move toward the road.

Gravel spews up against the bottom of the taxi. Soon we reach the outskirts of Bangkok. Multicolored houses with tin roofs sit along the wide street leading to downtown. Soon the streets begin to get crowded with cars and cycles and samlors. I get restless. I lean forward in my seat, watching the people going about their business. My hands begin to sweat. Ahead I can see the low skyline of the city.

Lieutenant Colonel Milligan...

We fly eastward. The low sun makes strange shadows across the morning landscape. Morning mist still clings to the greenery and to the wet terraced rice fields that stair-step up the sides of the mountains.

I think: The easiest way would be to say that it is a co-incidence. Then I could stop worrying about it and fly them as they come. Just wait until I'm done and go back to San Antonio with the wife and try to make a go of it again. I'll bet she's still as pretty as ever, the body still firm. A man tends to take his wife for granted over the years, but when you're away for a while you really miss these gals.

I adjust my airspeed. "Pinto lead throttling back," I say over the radio.

"Two, throttling," my number two man says.

"Three."

"Four."

It's tough on the gals, I think. Man away from home damn near half his career, or more. I look down at a small mountain village. The straw roofs are almost invisible against the ground. She was a nurse before we married, and damn fine. No nonsense. Kept the checkbook balanced while I was cashing checks all over creation—Japan, Korea, Hawaii, England and God knows where all. Did it without complaining. Almost raised the children single-handedly. Stayed a lowly lieutenant's wife for over seven years. Korea. And the Air Force gives precious little aid to these gals while their men are away.

The Air Force doesn't care. You're just a pawn in their game. I think a man who flies a three-million-dollar airplane should be paid as much, and accorded the respect of, a businessman who handles a three-million-dollar inventory every day. Especially a flight leader who has three charges with a payload in armament worth thousands that you have to lead over dangerous territory and back safe.

See, they'll never say it, but all they want to do is wait until you've got your time in so they can boot you out. You can bet your bottom dollar that they won't shed a tear when you go.

I check my fuel gauges. It's hard to see the gauges when you've been looking directly into the sun. The inside of the cockpit seems dark. I stare down until my eyes adjust. My shoulder harness is too tight. A little thing like that could mean a difference when you need all the flexibility available. I loosen the buckles on my shoulders. Then I wig-

114 · · ·

gle a little to see that the harness is not too loose. I reach around to make sure my D-ring is stowed properly. Fifty. Next month I'll be fifty years old.

Seems like the older you get, the more the Air Force looks over your shoulder, looking for an excuse to make you fly a desk for the rest of your career. They won't let a man do his job. Oh, no. Supervision and oversupervision. They tie your hands all along the line.

Sure, desk work has to be done, but there was a time when rank had its privileges. I could get a young shaver to fly the desk and I could get in more flight time. But Colonel Wright says Seventh Air Force is looking over his shoulder, and the Pentagon is looking over Seventh Air Force's shoulder, and Congress is looking over the Pentagon's shoulder, so where does that leave you? Any one of them would chop your neck off in a minute to save theirs, or give you easy missions. Lead the easy ones. Safe as flying over Texas for the old man. It simply proves, as I have contended, that the United States Air Force today doesn't give one iota about fighter-pilot experience. World War II was a young man's war.

A little of the haze beneath us seems to be burning off. "Pinto lead turning two degrees right," I say over the radio.

"Two, turning."

"Three."

"Four."

"Dolphin turning," McNaulty says. He is leader of the four-ship cell two thousand feet above us—the bastard.

"Dolphin 2, turning."

"Three."

"Four."

"Spare, turning," the spare says.

McNaulty might say I am turning too much, might say that the old man is nervous. I can see him telling Colonel Wright. That's all they sent him along for—to spy. See if the old man should be flying a desk instead of a jet. So they send you on an easy one—no Migs, no missiles, no big guns, just kids with rifles who can't bring you down even if they hit you. And then they send McNaulty along to spy. "Pinto lead, turning one degree left," I say over the radio. To hell with McNaulty.

"Two."

"Three."

"Four."

"Dolphin."

"Two."

"Three."

"Four."

"Spare."

McNaulty must be saying, "Why does the old bastard turn so much?" I see Ubon drifting by at about ten miles slant range off to the right. Right on course, I think. Ah-so! Right on course, McNaulty. The spare breaks off and goes home.

If I had something else to do, I'd get out next year. But a man retires from the service and in three years he's dead of a heart attack.

We come to the small hairpin turn in the Mekong River that isolates a sandy tidal island. The sun is on it. The mist has all burned away. We track toward it. I stiffen my face under my oxygen mask. Then we start across the wide part of Laos—about ten minutes wide. Green, hilly. Then we come to the mountainous indefinite border of South Vietnam. We turn north and after a moment the mountains begin to drop off beneath us. We seem to be going faster as the land goes downhill, speeding away from us until we are gliding a full fifteen thousand feet above the viny terrain cut by two small blue rivers.

I see the bend in the river on the right. The bend is a pointer to the village of Thanh Binh, the communist stronghold that we have to soften up before the ground troops move in. I take the boys down low. If you're going to pick up machine-gun fire, it's usually on the second pass. The first one is usually clean. I slide a napalm canister into the thick of things. Then I pitch up. I always have to marvel at these devils' power to survive. B-52's will hammer a village, but like a bunch of half-dead insects they drag the entire village up out of the bomb craters and start all over again, using the bomb craters as lakes. That's why napalm is better. Dolphin-lead and Dolphin 2 are working to the east of us in the woods. Dolphin 3 and 4 are working to the west, which leaves the four of us a mile-wide target-ingress and target-egress corridor which I split right down the middle because I know that McNaulty will be reporting to the Colonel as soon as he lands.

On the second run, I lay a CBU bomb down. No gunfire. By the third run we are simply laying the payload into the smoke and fire we have already made. I can't see the village. I wonder if the younger boys can see the village. They'll say they could even if they can't.

The fourth time, I hit the large embankment south of the village with a napalm canister so the fiery juice will splash up across the entire area. Then I wonder if the young fellows are going to claim that the old man can't see and is bombing short. I pull out. I come back across and see number 4 slam his napalm load into the side of the embankment. All of them must have caught on, I think.

Ah! They must have seen that it's better to hit on an incline than to hit in the flat of the village, where the splash of the juice will be attenuated by vertical objects.

There're no written techniques for napalm bombing, but that's where age and experience comes in, I think, and smile.

I think of how I'm going to be able to rib McNaulty at the Officers' Club. He never would have thought of that. That's why I say you can't find a substitute for experience— hit on an incline instead of on a flat surface. I come back across and lay my last CBU into the fire.

Ben...

I have to laugh at Damg because I still believe she's only pretending to be jealous. And me, with my suspicious self, begin wondering if the movies imitate the girls or are the girls imitating the movies. Two of them come past me, shading themselves with their kite-paper parasols, and just like in the movies, they glance back over their shoulders and expose one eye from under the parasol. Smiling, flirting with me. Then they turn and go.

There are so many foxy women in Bangkok that I halfway wish I had come alone. We go up the steps of the Wat Phra Keo, where Oriental spires stick up into the clear morning air like strange plants in an enchanted garden, but I cannot keep my mind on the brightly colored pagodas and dragons and steeples for looking at the women.

Ah, shit, I say to myself as we get to a landing where four girls are trying to take a picture of a GI friend. They laugh and pull at him and straighten his collar, adjust his head and his stance until they have him perfectly as they want him. Damg and I stop so we don't walk between the picture-takers and their subject. They snap one picture. One of the girls waves us pass. We go up the next set of stairs with me looking back at them.

An Indian family comes down the stairs; we move aside and go around under the shadow of a coral wall.

"Mock-mock beautiful," Damg says.

"When was it built?" I ask.

Damg looks in the booklet. She can read only a little English, and the booklet we picked up is in English and French because we assumed that I would be the one to read it. At the entrance to the Wat there were booklets in about ten languages. After we get out from under the shadow of the wall, we can see the river in front of us, the racecourse to the right, and the Temple of the Sleeping Buddha far away on the left.

I wonder why there could not be some kind of divine law that says men can only come to another man's country as tourists, and not as colonizers or exploiters. But when white men came to countries where people were just sitting on natural resources—just living and having babies and trying to be happy—they called them lazy or backward or uncivilized. They hated them and used them and justified whatever they did to them by invoking some kind of divine right of commerce. Discovered them, Christianized them, annihilated them or tried to make them into tools—hoes and cotton-pickers and brooms and shoeshine rags—for the great march of civilization.

Hard, chunky-walking, artless people who brought the whole world under their heels. We come back down into a courtyard. A girl in blue sits on the ground near a row of small spirit houses. I wait until Damg is not looking and wink at the girl. She winks back.

I like this city, I think, but there is the shadow of war hanging over it. And everywhere amid the Oriental spires are the signboards of American commercial dominance.

Stacy...

I sit on the edge of the concrete culvert that runs in front of the U.S.O. Club and the air-conditioned library trailer. Sweat is still coming off me from playing table tennis in the U.S.O. I look down toward the runway where they are testing two new F-111's. I read in the paper that they were bringing them over to try them at low level and during cloudy weather, when the F-105's are virtually useless.

For a moment I wonder what will happen if Ben means what he says about not flying any more. I didn't know what to say to him when he said it, but since then I have thought of a dozen things I should have said.

Two rescue helicopters hang like hummingbirds above the test operation. Past them the sky is empty above the ocean. The F-111's touch down, cob the engines, then slam the throttles forward, and take off again without stopping. They go off one after the other, heavy-looking in the hot air. They circle out over the water and come back and touch-and-go again, like they have been doing since before I went into the U.S.O. to play table tennis.

I wonder what the planes are like to fly. I've never been on a plane with retractable wings. I watch them touch-and-go again. I wouldn't mind flying one—anything that would help to end the war. B-58's, B-47's, whatever.

The Thai girls who are planting seeds in front of the new permanent quarters play more than they work. Ten of them are doing the work that three could do, which is probably why we pay them so little. But even so, they make more than most Thai people, which shows the advantages of the free-enterprise system. American Negroes make more than any nonwhite people on earth. I should have told Ben that, I think as I watch the planes touch-and-go again.

I knew there was something bothering him. It started as soon as he got over here. His personality was always three-quarters hidden. The side of the concrete culvert is rough against my bare heels. I am wearing shower clogs. I took them off and played table tennis barefooted. I think he would help his race more by doing the best he can over here and showing that a colored person can do the job as well as anyone.

I stare down into the culvert, where dirty water stands about an inch deep in irregular pools. I curl up my toes to make sure I don't drop my shower clogs into the dirty water. The hair on the back of my legs catches on the rough concrete. The dirty water comes down from where the Thai boys are washing the dust and dead insects off the buses. It never flows any farther than the concrete pipe, which looks ridiculously large during the dry season, but is not too large at all when monsoon rains come in May.

I don't think he'd give up a brilliant future—Harvard, Air Force officer, pilot—just like that; he'd be crazy. I look down at the pools of water and the bone-dry dust around them. He'll be all right after five days' rest. I know it's lonely being colored. He thinks too much. He seems to dwell on things, but it's lonely being a white man, too. I mean growing up to be one. You don't know which way to turn sometimes.

Across the culvert on the other side of the road the Thai men and women who work on the base are starting to come in to take their evening meal. I can't see the front of their shabby bamboo, tin and clapboard mess hall, but as soon as some of them get food they come out and sit in the shade of fan palms that grow along the road. Smoke comes up from the cooking fires and floats above the roof of the mess hall.

Their eating conditions are as dirty as hell. I hate this place, I think as I get up. I think about Roxanne as I head back toward my tent. I work a good image of her up in my mind so I can masturbate before going for a swim or something.

Ben...

"No, it's too much," Damg says. She grabs my arm before I can get my wallet out. Her voice rises. It always does when she's excited. "Don't pay that much for it," she says. The young Chinaman on the other side of the counter looks at her and smiles. She insists, "It's too much."

"Thirty-five, then," the Chinaman says. He smiles. His face is fleshy and smooth.

"Twenty-five," Damg says, feigning anger.

"Twenty-five?" He hits his forehead with the butt of his hand. "At twenty-five I *lose* money."

"Twenty, then," Damg says, and laughs. Then she says something in Thai or Chinese to the salesman's sister, who is standing near the window. They all laugh.

"Here. I give it to you. Eighteen-carat yellow gold. I give it to you," the salesman jokes, and tries to push the ring back on my pinky. His sister laughs and says something in Thai. I look at the ring. The yellow gold is beautiful with the black star sapphire setting and a row of white zircons along the edge of the main stone.

"Very good," Damg says, and pulls me toward the door.

"I go poorhouse," the salesman says, and starts toward the other door in the rear. He walks as if he is carrying luggage. "Okay, thirty dollar last price," he says as he comes back behind the counter.

My warm fingers make marks on the top of the glass display case. I examine the ring again. I like the heavy feel of it.

"Twenty-five," Damg says.

"Very tough bargainer," the salesman says to me, trying to get me to overrule her. "Thirty is good price. You say twenty, first price. I say forty, first price. Very good. I give it you thirty. Everybody happy." His round moon face melts into a smile.

Damg says something to him in Thai. He laughs in spite of himself. The sister laughs and then pulls the green velvet curtains back from the edge of the bottom of the display window so she can look out into the busy street. Heads pass above the curtain. Across the street, goldsmiths are working on a balcony surrounded by a wrought-iron banister.

The salesman's sister is tiny and beautiful. She knows I am looking at her. She smiles, accepting my admiration with modesty and poise. I bow my head slightly to her. "More tea?" she asks.

"Yes, please," I say. She takes my cup and leaves the room. An older woman sits in the corner, holding a baby in her arms. A Thai girl sits on a high stool behind the other counter, polishing large bronze chess pieces that look like the ones I sent Rose's brother at Cornell.

I look at some of the other jewelry in the long display counter, which covers almost the entire side of the small store. I think about how fast Damg grabbed my arm when I started to go for my money. Maybe I was on the verge of violating an Oriental custom. Maybe it's bad manners to show your money before both of you have settled on a price. Maybe they think that a deal is settled as soon as money is shown. I don't know. It could just be one of Damg's peculiarities.

I move back to the end of the counter, where Damg and the salesman are standing across from each other, looking down and pouting.

The salesman has one long hair cultivated on the tip of his chin. The fingernail of his pinky is long and curved, in the old style. I wonder if my fingernail would curve like that if I let it grow that long. "How much is something like this?" I say, taking his hand and holding up the cobra's-head ring he is wearing.

"Cheap," he says. "Fourteen-carat gold. This," he points to the ring that Damg wants me to buy for myself, "eighteen-carat gold, is much better. Gold, number one. Dollar, number ten. You give me dollar, I give you gold." He holds a smile on his plump face. "Yellow gold is very pretty on doom-doom puchi." Again his face melts into a happy uncomplicated smile.

I wonder is he sorry that I brought Damg along. She's still looking at the counter, pouting. He tries to ignore her by talking to me. I wonder how much money Damg has saved me today. She helped me shop for the things to send home to my wife and then for a ring to send to the girl I was fucking in Nevada. She seemed to show no jealousy and she bargained as hard as she is bargaining now. She got me to get a white silk Italian-cut suit with high buttons in the front and a purple lining, which I never would have had the nerve to buy for myself, and it would have cost me twice as much as forty-five dollars.

I think about the suit. I can pick it up from the tailor's at five o'clock.

It's the first flashy suit I've ever owned. I've always gone around with a hundred-thousand-dollar education in my head and ten-dollar suits on my back. The sister comes back with the tea. A large Siamese cat follows her through the green curtains. "Okay," the brother says," I give you the ring: eighteen-carat gold, with black star sapphire setting, and a gold tie clip, all for forty dollar." He does not look at Damg. I put sugar in my tea. I look at Damg. She shakes her head. I say, "Okay."

Then I buy some silk for Damg's stepmother and a bronze incense-burner for her half-sister who lives in Thonburi near the railway station. A Thai servant takes all the things we bought to the rear and returns soon with them wrapped in small neat packages. The packages are put in a black cellophane shopping bag. We leave the store and go down Rama Road looking for a place to get a cool drink. I order beer and Damg orders Coke on the patio at the Lumpini.

She drinks her Coke through a red-and-white straw. Her hair falls from in back of her shoulders.

Her hands are small on the glass. She slurs the last of the Coke from the ice chips at the bottom. I wonder how long it will be before the war turns Bangkok to rubble. They'll give the war some noble rationale, like calling it a war to save the freedom-loving people of Thailand.

I remember the large Bulova Watch sign towering

above Sukhumwit Road, and the Texaco signs on the road into the city. When the war comes to Thailand it will be this that American troops will be brought here to defend. I think about prison.

My stomach knots up again. I wonder why the greedy motherfucker can't leave other people alone.

Lieutenant Colonel Milligan...

My strides are bigger because I feel good. I dig my
heels into the soft sand between the tents. A man is bound
to feel better after he's done the job, and done it well. A
man will stand differently, walk prouder, see the world in a
different manner. The base looks not half-bad as I come
down the row between the tents in the twilight.

I think about McNaulty, and smile. He'll just have to
hear it tonight, because I feel like giving it to him. And he
can stand and take it, or leave the Club.

The base is laid out wrong though, I think. The officers'
tents are up against the jungle with the beach hooking
around behind them. The rest of the base is on a lower por-
tion of the peninsula, and the ocean hooks around again on

the other side of the runway, which runs parallel to the base.

Officers' quarters should sit right where the enlisted men's quarters are, so *we* would be surrounded on three sides by the water.

I feel that Thailand is not half-bad this evening. Sure it's not as dirty as Korea, or even North Africa, but I'd rather be in North Africa because on a weekend you can jump right over to France and spend a couple of clean days. A light wind comes off the flight line, bringing the sound of jet engines from down on the test-stands near the ammo dump. The bright lights along the runway look more military than anything else around here. I can see the roofs of the rest of the base. The olive tent-tops look drab and lifeless, and the few wooden structures look even worse. We've got a long way to go over here, but if you come back in two years, you won't recognize the place. You'll wonder how they did it. They'll put up a two-billion-dollar permanent establishment in less than two years, you watch.

I put a little skip in my walk to overtake a young troop coming out of one of the latrines, leaning forward zipping up his fly. "It's a scorcher," I say.

"Wh-e-e," he says. He looks and sees that I am Colonel Milligan. Most of the young troops know who I am. I try to talk a lot to some of the younger troops to get their ideas on things.

"It'll be hotter tomorrow," I say. "Heading for the Officers' Club?"

"Yes, sir," he says. We go in single file across the wooden footbridge that separates the officers' quarters from the rest of the base. From behind, the troop looks a little overweight. Probably a ground troop, but that's important too. Even the lowliest little librarian is part of the aerospace team. But you can tell the flying troops from the others—more spring in their walk, prouder carriage.

But one of the important functions of command is to let every troop know that his job is important. We go down between the base legal office and the chapel.

"Can't wait to get to the bar and get that first cold one, huh?" I say.

"I can almost taste it," he says. He has a wide, soft face. A lot of the younger troops are softer than we were.

"One of these days this will be one of the finest military establishments in the world," I say. "It will be a symbol of American presence in Southeast Asia." I squint as we walk, trying to imagine how the base will look when all the canvas and wood has been replaced by steel and brick. Then all the roads will be paved. Grass. Maybe a few houses for the families of the permanent-party troops. "They couldn't have picked a better location. I was born in the middle of Texas, but I believe I have the ocean in my blood. And I bet before the Americans came, the Thais weren't fully utilizing this piece of real estate, probably didn't really see the full potential in it."

"It's a nice location," the young troop says.

"It has potential. God knows, all of Thailand has potential—a proud nation. All they need is a little Yankee know-how." I clench my teeth. "The Thai people have much in common with the American people. Though you might think at first that it's the Japanese. The Japanese get things done. Industrious. But the Thais have never been conquered. That's a distinction they share with us alone.

"Yes, sir," the young man says, and quickens his pace.

I wonder if I am talking too much. I decide to give the troop a chance to get some of his ideas out.

"Can you think of another people who have never been conquered?"

He shakes his head.

"The Vietnamese, they've had the hell kicked out of them by the French and then the Japs and then the French again," I whisper. "Corruption is rampant. We don't really give a damn about them. They're a lost race of people. Who we care about are the Thais. We want to set up a buffer between them and the Chinese," I say. The young troop quickens his pace again. Sometimes many of the young troops refuse to look at the big picture. All they want to do is get their hitch done and go home, but they don't realize that it's because of people like me that they have homes to go to. They'd all be eating rice and chop suey next year if somebody didn't care. "If Thailand falls, by God, the Philippines will be next, and then Burma, and then Australia, then Hawaii, then, by God, California," I clench my teeth to emphasize what I'm saying.

He speeds up, but I stay right with him. "There are six hundred billion of those Chinks," I say. "Think of that, six hundred billion of those bastards out to get us."

He speeds up again. "Can you imagine that many people marching across the ocean . . ."

"Six hundred million, sir."

"What?" We go past the post office.

"Six hundred million."

"Oh, what did I say?"

"Six hundred billion."

I laugh. I can see that he is getting irritated—so will McNaulty—but I'm going to keep giving it to him anyway. "Well, all I know is there are more of them than there are of us." I laugh. "We don't know how many there are. The Chink Government don't know. We're working on a satellite right now that will count them. Until then nobody knows," I say abruptly.

"We're not fighting the Chinese," he says in the same abrupt tone of voice.

"Ah! That's what a lot of young troops don't comprehend. Take it from an old soldier. I have more time in the military than you got in this world. If you kick the hell out of the little dog, you won't have as much trouble with the big one. China's the big one. Six hundred billion of those fuckers, and they're growing. They say a Chinese woman can have a baby in seven months."

"That's not true," he says. "I'm a doctor and that's just not true."

"We don't know for sure. They call Asia the dark continent . . . A doctor, that's where I've seen you. In the flight surgeon's office."

"No, I'm in public health. I was a public-health administrator. We're over here designing an orphanage for children of Thai women and American servicemen," he says.

"Is that so?" I wrinkle my brow. "I didn't know that. Where are you from?"

"New York," he says. He is a little angry, but who cares.

"Children?"

"Two."

"New York is a beautiful city."

"I'm from Long Island."

"I have two fine boys myself, both of them in college. I couldn't retire now if I wanted to." The young troop is almost running. I run along with him. Other troops are coming from different directions heading for the club. I slow down and file this young doctor's insubordinate soft face away in my memory for future reference. The Officers' Club is noisy. I head straight for the stag bar, looking for McNaulty.

Ben...

We passed more night clubs along this one street than I have ever seen in any single place in my life. We walk faster as we get nearer the most crowded part. The more beautiful women I see the more excited I get. Music pours out the doors to mix with the strange Oriental sounds of the hawkers selling sweets and flowers on the other side of Phet Buri Road.

The neon signs make the area as bright as the Ginza on a shopping night or Times Square in the summertime. Damg and I step out in the street to get past the groups of GI's and their girls flooding the sidewalks and rushing in and out of the clubs.

The small neon signs in English, Thai and Chinese jut out over the crowded walks. The SUNFLOWER BAR. The CASANOVA, with blinking green lights above a blue sign. The CASBAR. THE RAVEN CLUB, with a large raven flapping his red neon wings against a black window. The door is open. I peep inside. Crowded. Across the street sits the Club 69. I look again. Club 69, bigger than shit. I laugh. We walk out in the street past a squad of black Marines and their girls. The girls look like Koreans. Tall. The Marines are harmonizing like the Five Royales as they bop down the sidewalk.

THE PING PONG CLUB. Next to it is the THAI PARADISE that you have to go down five steps to get to. A blinking arrow points the way. I feel like singing too. I almost wish I had come into the service as an enlisted man so I'd have some black guys to hang around with. Childress and I were never very close. The inside of the Hong Kong Club looks interesting. More women than men. I hold the door open. Damg says, "No, I know a place which is much better."

We go past the Sweet Dream, which has an outdoor garden in front where you can sit out on stone benches and watch the girls flow by. "I know number one place," Damg says.

"Okay, baby. You know more than I do," I say. Damg worked in Bangkok for two years as a massage girl. She came from up-country when she was fifteen to work as a house servant for a rich Japanese family. They took her to Tokyo for a while. From them she learned to speak English, and an older servant in the household taught her the Japanese style of massage, which gave her a good way to make a living when the family left Bangkok for Singapore and she decided not to go with them because she didn't want to live outside Thailand for long. I asked her once. "You come U. S. with me?"

She said, "No, I have my family in Thailand. My friends are here. I love Thailand. You stay Thailand. I make you good wife."

"America is nice," I said.

"America have no love," she said. She adored John Kennedy. He was assassinated while she was living with Sergeant Hadley. For more than a month after the assassination Hadley said she spit every time someone mentioned America.

A group of young white GI's come down the sidewalk like a gang of high school boys, talking loud, trying to give each other the courage to go get some girls. The oldest one looks about seventeen. He is tall and redheaded, with ears like LBJ's. "Old Burdett doesn't know what he's talking about," Red says, turning sideways as he walks.

Damg pulls me into the Lance-A-Lot Club. My eyes adjust slowly to the darkness. The place is crowded and noisy. Only the bandstand is lighted well. The spotlight is on the lead singer, who is the fattest Oriental I have ever seen. His too-small shirt is wet with sweat. His hair is pasted to the side of his head and his eyes are closed as he croons into the microphone, trying to sing like Wilson Pickett:

> I found a love,
> I found a love,
> I found the love,
> That I ne-e-ed

Three normal-sized Thais sing the refrain:

> Yea-a, Ye-a-a-a
> Ye-a, Ye-a-a-a-ah
> That I need.

We stand near the door for a moment. Not far from us a black GI in a silk dashiki holds a cane to his mouth, pretending he is singing into a microphone. His face is contorted with passion. His head bobs to the music. The handle of the cane is shaped like the head of a dragon. His eyes are closed and he is screaming into the face of the dragon: "I found a love, I found a love." He holds the cane down and sings down to it, "I found the love, that I need."

I laugh.

Damg and I dance. Her purse hangs from her arm. She tries to roll her body into me. I buckle my knees and roll back into her. I can't pick up her earnest little rhythm, so I hug her tight and make her pick up mine. Over her shoulders I see other GI's bending to get down with the short girls. I know now how it would feel if I were six foot five back in the States. I wonder how Childress and Damg made out. I think about Wilt Chamberlain. I feel like a Watusi as I rub myself lightly across her.

> And when I call her
> In the midnight hour.
> She says, Yea-a, Ye-a-a-a-a
> She says, Yea-a, Ye-a-a-a-a-aH
> That I need.

The fat singer's name is painted on the bass drum: "Big Buddha and His . . ." The other words are hidden by a trumpet case.

The bar is at the far end of the narrow room. We dance directly in front of the bandstand, which is in the center against the wall. The trumpet player blows hard and off-key. When he puts his horn down to sing the refrain, I ream out my ear.

Waiters move among the tables with trays of drinks held high above their heads. Big Buddha's trousers hang low on his hips. His eyes roll around in their sockets as he moans. Then he raises his hand and snaps it downward for the band to stop.

I say, "Go 'head, Big Buddha."

We move around in the crowd, looking for vacant tables, but before we find one Big Buddha starts a fast number. We crowd back out on the small dance floor.

"Go 'head, Big Buddha," I yell, and laugh. "Go 'head with yo' bad self."

A black GI near me laughs. "Buddha is into his shit, ain't he?"

"Ain't he?" I say. I pull my sweating shirt away from me.

"If Big Buddha does a James Brown number, I'm gonna fall out," the GI says.

"Shit! You? *Me*. They gon' have to carry me out."

"I know what you mean." He laughs. There is a big new gold tooth sitting right in the center of his laughing mouth. After the fast number we go and sit with the GI and his girl. His girl is round-faced and almost as dark as I am. She laughs more than Damg does, probably because she can't speak English.

Stacy...

I wake up and look over at Ben's cot. The tent seems completely empty with both of them gone. Before, one of them was always here, or I could lay awake and think that one of them would soon come back from town or from a flight. I stare at the empty beds. I wonder why they didn't put someone new in Childress' place after he left. I stare at the thin coat of dust that collects in only a few hours on the red floorboards under the beds. I think about Ben.

Everything seems to matter more than it did, I think, continuing something I had been half-thinking and half-dreaming while I was tossing around in the heat last night. I remember how my eyes came open several times, and when they were closed, they were closed simply because I was forcing them to stay closed. Ben's words were like lights turned on inside my head. All night they glowed dully there, keeping me awake and tossing, and when I opened my eyes things were darker than they were with my eyes closed.

He said, "I'm not going to fly any more." I could hear

his voice. I could almost see him, and I kept wondering how much hatred there was hidden in him.

I get up and walk to the screen door and look out at the dull tent-tops, sitting like olive-colored, well-shaped turds in the dust between the ocean and the jungle.

I don't see why he would throw away his future like that. They'll almost have to send him to prison. I come back to the bed and slip my feet into my shower clogs and start across the sand to the showerhouse. The screen door slams behind me. Already the day is hot. The sun burns my naked back. I retie the towel around my waist and walk toes-up.

There's no telling how much he could accomplish with a background like his. He could work his way up to $50,000 a year in no time flat. A Harvard grad, a jet pilot, combat time.

I turn the water on and step under the cold stream. It feels good. I let it run down across my shoulders for a while, then I turn around and open my mouth and gargle as the cold water flows into it. He could write his own ticket, I think. Ben, goddamnit. Don't be so full of self-pity and self-righteousness. I want out of this mess. Shit, everything is falling apart.

Someone comes into the latrinepart of the shower-house. I stop thinking until they leave. I hear someone whistling outside. I stand out from under the water and soap myself. I raise lather in the hair on my legs. Then I stick my right leg under the shower and let the water pull the soap off, then the left leg. I can't get Ben off my mind. I re-soap myself and then get under the cold water again. Instead of relaxing, my body gets tight and I start to shiver.

Maybe I should go to the beach and take a good long

swim, I think. I almost wish that I was flying today. I go back to the tent and stand close to my locker as I pull my green swim trunks up on me. The sun is hotter as I start across base. I think you sweat more after you've been under a cold shower. My swim trunks are tight, cutting. I walk wide-legged down the narrow path, which widens out suddenly as the ocean becomes visible. The surface of the water stretches more white than blue toward the edge of the blue sky, where clouds are beginning to form.

I see some of the guys from the squadron lounging under a straw sunshade that looks like a large coolie's hat perched on a thin bamboo pole. If I don't go over and sit with them, they'll call me a snob. They already think I'm strange anyway for rooming with two darkies. I should've roomed with two white guys. The tour would have gone faster. I should've stayed with my own kind.

"Where's your roomie?" Harwood asks. He is laying on a green towel, with his face in the shade. His chest is oily with suntan lotion.

"Bangkok," I say, and spread my towel out near Barker's feet.

"With that same girl?" Barker asks. Barker is pudgy. He is sitting with his legs spread straight in front of him. A high wave of chestnut-colored hair sits on top of his head. It looks silly because the sides of his head are very closely cropped. He smiles like Woody Woodpecker, with his hooked nose. I pick up my towel and smooth out the sand, then lay it down again. I wonder should I tell them about Ben.

"That gal's made a fortune off those two niggers," Harwood says, and laughs. His face is narrow, sallow. He needs a shave. I lay down.

"Darkies love it over here," Captain Fitzhugh says. I hate the word nigger. I like darkie better, but I wouldn't say either out in public. I look down the beach to where the Thai village is, but I continue to listen.

"I'd like to smuggle a couple of them gals back to Harlem. I'd make me a fortune. Two dollars a throw," Harwood says. Everybody laughs. I don't look at their faces. Barker lays his cigar on the edge of a beer can. It smokes over the wedge-shaped opening on the top of the can. Then he picks it up and thrusts the soggy end into his mouth. "Ben's got a cute little wife, though. She was out at Nellis with him for a while," Barker says timidly. Everyone is almost afraid of Harwood.

"Niggers and Asians get along like peas in a pod," Captain Fitzhugh says. "Bringing niggers over here is like sliding turds into a greasy pool. Pluoop!" He laughs hard and lays down, bringing his hands up and across his eyes as the sun hits his face.

"Thai women are sure better-looking than the stuff they got at home," Harwood says.

I don't say anything. Perhaps Ben does hate us. If I were feeling better, I would tell them all to shut their mouths. I could beat all their asses put together. I'd kick Harwood's ass first.

Lieutenant Bordreau raises his head on his hands. "Wait just one cotton-picking minute. The colored women you Yankees got up North are things we didn't want down South. Why, you should see some of the sweet colored gals we got in Atlanta and Washington and New Orleans," he says.

"Might know Bordreau would say that. He's in love with one. Got her picture on his locker. The hussy won't write him though," Fitzhugh says. Everyone laughs. I look at them.

"She's nice, I gar-and-damn-tee you that. I think every red-blooded American boy should fall in love with one before he settles down to a thirty-year mortgage and twin beds," Bordreau says.

"Why doesn't the wench write you, then?" Fitzhugh says.

"I don't like the way they smell, myself," Harwood says.

"Shit, you Yankees worship the germ theory. Whatever ain't white ain't clean. All ya'll want to do is eat it anyway," Bordreau says, and runs off toward the water. "Fuck all you limp-dick Yankees."

"He'd have to say that, as many nights as he spends downtown," Harwood says.

I get up and head for the water too. I should have roomed with Bordreau and only one darkie, I think.

Dang...

We are not tired from walking. We make love all night. Something is worrying him which he will not tell me about.

When I give him a massage I ask him what, but he say nothing. I do not know.

I lay on my side against him and know that he still wants to make love to me because he is still large between my legs. His breath is soft but very deep. I pull him over on top of me again.

He holds his arms along my sides like braces. His elbows are on my hips, giving me his rhythm. His hands, spread against my back, hold me close to him as he comes into me slowly and uses his arms and elbows and hands to give me his rhythm until it is good.

Soon he squeezes his elbows in on top of my hips to give me another rhythm, which is different than the rhythm of his hips as he comes down into me. His legs are hard like the limbs of an ironwood tree between mine.

I feel him straining himself, but he is gentle to me,

keeping himself from coming too far down into me by keeping his elbows squeezed in between our hips. His sweat comes down on me. I reach up and put my hands into the wool of his hair, which is soft when he is sweating.

His breath is hot against the pillow and the side of my face. I massage his back. Then he moves his elbows from between us and I cup my heels behind his ass to bring him all the way into me. I hold him into me for a long time and massage his back until everything comes out of him. He moans. I am quiet, as a woman must be, as joy comes over me.

Ben...

The propeller is turning deep under water. It makes a slight ripple behind us on the surface of the Chao Phraya River. I watch the rippled, misty water and wonder what am I going to do

I stare for a long time. Then I look up at our boatman. He swings the propeller pole to the left. The nose of the boat moves to the right, away from a hand-paddled boat stacked high with fresh fruits and vegetables. A wrinkled old woman in a black dress rows the small boat toward the mouth of the canal. We follow. I am tired from making love, but I still want to hold someone and make love again. Damg will never understand why I don't want to be away from someone. She sits near the front of the boat. I step forward carefully and sit down beside her.

Along the river other boats loaded with produce and food for the floating market rock in the wakes made by the motor-launches taking passengers across the river from Bangkok to Thonburi. Sampan traffic is heavy. A long raft made from cords of strapped-together teakwood moves slowly in the mist behind us. The teakwood is forested in the hill country and takes about a year to float downstream to the mills around Bangkok. A little attap hut sits on top of the raft. A logger, and perhaps his entire family, lives in the hut during the year-long journey.

I stare at the tiny hut. Tomorrow I will have to go back to base to face charges, I think. The canal narrows. I can't think straight.

Along the shores monks in saffron robes move among the houses, collecting food. Small boats push toward the shore to sell food and provisions to the women who come down to the water's edge, and to the others who live along the water and simply have to step out on the veranda to buy the things they need from the floating market. I watch the small merchant boats jockey for position.

Then I think about Damg. If I had told her I wanted to stay in bed, she would have stayed, but she cannot understand how desperate I am. The tone of the motor deepens as we go slower.

"Kei Mau?" Damg asks.

"Nit noy," I answer, smiling. She is too close to see me smile. I put my face against her hair. My chin is smooth where she shaved it.

Then Damg buys noodles and fish-sauce from two boys in a boat that has rubber tires for bumpers. The oldest boy ladles the fish-sauce over the noodles. The warm food tastes good in the cool misty air. A Thai family bathes in the brown water. The mother soaps her back. She has a loosely fitted wrap around her and she soaps herself under the wrap. Two naked children swim and bathe themselves in

the water near her. For a moment soapsuds float on top of
the water. A small boy pees from his veranda into the river
near the family.

The sun comes up slowly on the horizon ahead of us. It
shines down the long narrow corridor that the canal cuts between the houses and pale trees. I push my coolie's hat
down over my eyes and continue eating.

"Doom-doom puchi needs sunglasses," Damg says to
the boatman. Then she says something to him in Thai. I
point upstream.

"No have," I finally say.

"No sweat, I buy," she says. I give her a dollar. The
traffic thins out and we come to a place where children are
playing ball in the water. We nudge through the crowd of
them. Sometimes their black heads look like the noses of
dolphins bobbing to the surface. Three boys grab our boy.
The boy tows them for a short while until one of them falls
off. The other two hang on, oblivious to the dangerous propeller churning a few feet below them.

"Thai fish," Damg says, and laughs.

They ride for a long time. Their thick straight hair is
plastered to the sides of their brown heads. The water flows
into smiling mouths as the boys bounce about in the waves
our boat is making.

Soon they drop off. Damg says something to the boatman in Thai. We all turn to watch the boys swim back
toward their companions. Then the boatman moves the pro-
peller-pole to the left and our boat moves toward the right
shore. He pushes the pole down. The propeller comes up
out of the water. We drift the rest of the way to dockside.
Damg gets off and disappears into the small shop at the rear

of the wooden dock. In a moment she comes back with sunglasses for me. The boat rocks as she steps in. I put the glasses on.

Damg looks. "I like," she says.

I turn so the boatman can see. "Number one," he says. He pushes the boat off from the dock with his foot. He says something to another water taxi driver as he winds the rope around the shaft to start the motor. They both look at me and smile.

"Thai people like you," Damg says. "He say you samesame Thai people. American Negro," Damg says to the other driver.

"Chi," the old man says. He is very skinny. I put my palms together and make a wai to him. Carved on the prow of his boat is the head of a laughing dragon.

Damg takes a seat far to the front of the boat, and as we move out into mid-canal again she begins to look forward. I watch the back of her head and think about her. Her small legs are folded back under her on the seat. She turns, "When I be a rich woman, I buy a house like that." She points to the roof of a large house back among the pale green trees. It is almost invisible among the flat palm branches.

"Are you still saving money?"

"Chi," she smiles, and turns around. She seems very fragile, and I think about making love to her and how gentle I have to be. We made love yesterday, but for some reason it didn't feel as good. Daylight was coming in through the gauzy curtains into the hotel room. I kept trying to keep my eyes closed against it, but whenever I would have to open them I would get an impression of hard gauzy light on my mind, and it would stay there.

I kept thinking about my wife, wondering what she will do. Damg's hands were small on my back. My wife's hands are larger, plumper, stronger, with longer fingers. Damg's hair fits flat to her head and I could feel the contours of her skull beneath. I remembered the smell of the pomade my wife used. Her hair was greased and hot-combed before I left. I have never made love to a woman with an Afro and I kept wondering what it would be like. I'd push my head sideways, as if I were pushing it into the frizzly fluff of Rose's hair, but pretty soon I would feel the reminding contours of Damg's skull. Her legs were soft and small and she was silent making love. Rose moaned and called, "Oh, Lord, oh, Lord, oh, Lord." Damg remains silent and her body becomes rigid beneath me just before she climaxes with a quick jerk and a little whimper.

Making love was nicer at night. The light was softer, and I, over my quick excitement, could stay with her for a while and enjoy being with her. Between times we sat naked in the bed, and before long the sight of the perfect curves of her soft brown body would make me want her again. Her skin was smooth, without one blemish to the eye, and it was shiny-feeling against my own skin.

The sun warms me and gradually I forget about the bed. I begin to think about tomorrow again. I begin to wonder again what will happen.

Stacy...

"Where in the world are you taking me?" I giggle. The night is hot. We have walked a long way in the heat.

"I was lucky to get you off base at all," Bordreau says.

"I needed another beer."

"They've got beer. Ice-cold. This is a high-class establishment."

"It looks like it," I say, as we come down the path so narrow that we have to push overhanging branches out of our way as we walk.

"Nothing but the best," Bordreau says.

"Then why do they have to hide it back here?"

"We're not that far. Watch. We're right at the back-door to the base. Korean girls, man. Tall, cynical, high cheekbones.

"I don't care about the girls, all I want is a cold beer."

"I told you I'd find you one. No matter what time of day or night your boy Bordreau'll look out for you."

Soon we come into view of the runway lights. "Right in back of the base."

"Would I shit you? Why don't you try a girl? I'll pay for it."

"That's okay. I'll drink my beer and wait for you."

"You still a virgin, huh?"

I giggle. Through the trees we can see the clearing just before you get to the high chainlink fence that encircles the base. The flight-line lights are aimed the other way.

"I bet I could make a million dollars if I could get a couple of white whores over here. They got a place in Bangkok," Bordreau says.

"I'd pay just to talk to a white woman about now," I say. The path turns a little away from the base. "How long you going to be?" I giggle.

"No sooner than you finish two beers, I'll be finished."

"A quickie."

"I don't mess around out here. I forgot to tell you, this place is illegal." He laughs.

"Oh, shit." I giggle.

"Don't worry."

"What gives?" We come in sight of two small compounds in a clearing in the trees. From the other side the compounds can be reached by a narrow road that goes up a short hill.

"There's a little mess going on back here. I don't know. And it stays open after hours."

We step up on a wooden walkway. Light comes through the cracks in the wall of the first compound. A Thai boy sits near a bamboo door. He gets up and opens it as we approach. He bows from the waist. Inside, the floor is concrete and the center of the compound is open to the stars. A raffia awning extends from all four sides of the place. Tables, chairs and two bars sit under the awnings. The place is lighted by candles. GI's and their girls sit without saying much. The girls look at us as we come in. The place gives me a funny feeling.

"Papa-san," Bordreau says. A fat Oriental in a tee-shirt comes toward us.

He bows and says, "Sawadee."

Bordreau takes his hands in both of his own. "How are you?"

"Fine, Mr. Lieutenant," the man says, smiling.

"This is my friend, Lieutenant Stacy."

"Sawadee."

"Sawadee," I say.

"What for you?" he asks Bordreau. I look around.

"Is she here?"

"She wait for you, Mr. Lieutenant."

"What for your friend? Something special?"

I look at the man again. The smile never leaves his face. "Just a beer."

"Very good," he says. A lot of the GI's and girls are nodding like they are sleepy. Flames on the candles stand straight up. There is no breeze at all in this compound. I feel like I am going to suffocate.

"Hey, sit down and have a beer. I'll be with you in a minute," Bordreau says.

"Yes," the old man says, "maybe you will have something better later." He grins disgustingly. There is the still smell of rot or mildew in the air. I sit at a vacant end of the bar. A tall girl in a blue floor-length silk gown comes toward me. The host waves her away. Then he goes to the back of the other bar and serves up a beer. A small boy brings it to me. He drags his sandals on the concrete floor. Bordreau disappears into a small doorway. I drink the beer slowly. The silence is depressing. I sit for a moment and then I see a small girl pulling on the arm of a blond GI at the bar across on the other side. "Speak Thai," she says.

He says, "But I love you and I want to take you back to Duluth."

She keeps pulling on his arm, screeching, "Speak Thai."

He tries to say something in Thai, then he retreats to English. "I want you to be with me."

The girl is angry with him. She pouts. He says something in Thai and then leans over and tries to kiss her. She moves out of the way quickly. He almost falls off the bar stool.

I hear the sound of a plane. I look up and the sky is empty, but the plane sounds like it is almost directly overhead, low like it is just taking off. The walls vibrate a little and the candle flames shake. A girl comes out of the doorway which Bordreau entered awhile ago. She is walking on the back of her heels. Not until she has almost crossed the compound do I see that she is pregnant. I want to get up and leave, but also I want to wait for Bordreau to talk to him on the way back. Candlelight shows in the windows of some of the rooms along the four walls of the compound. Some of them are covered with mosquito nets. Two tall girls dance with each other in an archway to the left.

I order another beer and drink it slowly. After some time Bordreau comes out pulling his hair straight back on his head. I leave a dollar on the counter and we go out. We walk for a while without saying anything. Then I say, "What the hell was going on in there? That place was spooky."

"Opium, mostly," he says, and looks at me.

"Then what the hell are you doing down here? What were the GI's doing?"

"Most of them are on it. Most of the ones who come here. Most of the girls.

"You?"

"No. The girl I met is."

"Why . . . ?"

"I don't know. I just like to come here. I like her. She speaks perfect English. I don't know, Stacy. I wanted you to see it, though."

"Why don't you turn them in, for God's sake?"

"I don't know."

We walk slowly. "You're not doing them any favor by not turning them in."

"I know. A lot of them are very young. Can't adjust to the war," he says. We stop and watch two planes make downwind takeoffs. They come almost directly overhead. The bomb and underbelly tank look like the bloated belly of a frog beneath the streamlined body. "You're still a virgin, right?"

I don't say anything.

"There're a lot of contradictions in the world. You know a lot of the kids in there on opium have never slept with a woman. That's the truth. For all we know, one of those pilots might be a virgin. I don't know what the fuck we're doing over here, a bunch of self-righteous bastards like us. You know?"

"We have a commitment," I say, and stiffen my lip.

"What the fuck does that mean?"

"Just that we have to stay until the fight is over. Otherwise our word wouldn't be worth a nickel."

"That's easy to say when we're over here tearing up someone else's country. We wouldn't feel the same way if it was our country, our children."

"That's what we're trying to prevent."

"Yeah, and that's what I don't like about it."

"Self-preservation is the first law of nature."

"What are we going to do, fuck with everybody on earth that might be a potential threat to us?"

"If we have to." I stiffen my lip and push a branch out from in front of me. I stoop a little under another branch.

"Yeah, the only thing is, we can't. The odds are running out. We fucked with too many people."

"After what I saw tonight, I think we ought to level the entire continent and start all over again."

He looks at me as if he doesn't believe I meant what I said. "Look out for our own ass; if we don't nobody will."

"I think we're a bunch of imperialist bastards. We've built a dike around our loved ones and folks. The dike keeps springing leaks and we've only got ten fingers to plug them up. What happens when the dike springs the eleventh hole?"

I laugh. "You're beginning to talk like Ben."

"Why? What does Ben say?"

I stop walking. "Ben says he's not going to fly any more."

"Yeah? What did Colonel Milligan say?"

"He doesn't know yet."

"Then who knows?"

"Nobody." I pick up a vine and start to chew it. "He's in Bangkok now. He'll be back day after tomorrow."

"Damn, I know how he feels."

"He won't fly any more. I know him."

"It's easier for him to do something like that. I mean, being black, it's easier for him."

"I don't believe anybody should give up in the middle of a fight." We do not say anything until we near the main road.

"Hey, you can probably make it back to base from here. I think I'm going back to see Kim."

"Yeah, okay. If that's the way you want it," I say. I walk up to the road and then turn and see him retreating into the trees. "You believe like you want to believe and I believe like I want to," I say to myself as if I were talking to him.

Lieutenant Colonel Milligan...

I thank God that no matter how much I drink I never get a hangover. I go across the hot sand toward the showerhouse. The sun is always nicest early in the morning. God, this is beautiful country—raw beauty, majestic jungle.

I think about McNaulty. He *was* mad. So mad he had to leave the club last night. I smile. The showerhouse is empty. I put my soap dish and toothpaste on the red board under the mirror. Then I turn the water on and watch it splash into the white porcelain face bowl. I wonder if there'd be some way to make convertible roofs on these showerhouses, so you can get sunlight inside when you want it.

Moss is on my tongue from drinking gin, but no hangover. McNaulty *was mad*. I almost laugh out loud. I squeeze toothpaste on my brush. I hate to think of how it will taste on my mossy tongue. When I retire I should get a job at a toothpaste factory. I'd invent a toothpaste that'd make your mouth feel clean without making it sweet or antiseptic. Knowing industry, they've probably got some Ph.D. scientist working on it, which proves that a little common sense is sometimes better than a lot of education.

If they write up my procedure I'll be known throughout the Air Force as "The Man Who Invented the Splash Technique." McNaulty couldn't take the ribbing. I laugh.

On that basis, maybe a toothpaste factory would hire me as an applied scientist. I'd invent a toothpaste that tastes like a good clean tomato, or an apple. You could put it in the refrigerator, get it out each morning, and it would make your mouth feel fresher than this stuff ever will.

I slide the toothbrush into my mouth. Then I stare into the mirror. Nothing ventured, nothing gained, I think. And maybe it would work. By God, it just might.

Then I think about the matters pending at the office. That's why I would rather fly almost every day. I hate desk work.

Stacy...

Milligan's office is small and dim. One small window
high in the wall gives light above the yellowish fluorescent
lamp on his desk. I wonder if he has called me in to talk
about Ben. I decide that I'm not going to tell him anything.
I watch him as he adjusts some papers on his desk.

Behind him a colored picture of his wife and two sons
sit on a two-by-four crossbeam against the rough unpainted
wall. "I'd like to ask you a few questions about Lieutenant
Benjamin Williams," he says, sure enough. I brace myself. A
youngish man in civilian clothing sits on a side table under
the window. "Frankly, we want to determine if Lieutenant
Williams is a communist." He lays his hands out flat on the
desk top. He does not take his eyes off me.

I pause. "I don't think he is," I say. "No, I'm sure he's
not." I look at the civilian, but he is not looking at us. He is
below the light that comes in the window. I cannot see his
face well.

"Are you quite sure?" the Colonel says. The skin on his

face is leathery from too much sun. Fluorescent light makes it look dead.

"I don't know," I say, and cross my legs, trying to relax. The man in civilian clothes is still not looking at us. Milligan reaches into his desk, fumbles for a moment, then pulls something out.

"Do you know a Miss Damgsen Tasuri?" he asks.

"Yes, I've heard of her. I mean, I know who she is." My stomach tightens more. So that's what it is, I think.

"Through Lieutenant Williams?"

"Yes."

"Yes, well, we have strong reason to suspect her of being a communist agent."

I do not move.

"She is very beautiful?"

"I think so."

"And is it true that she dates only Negro GI's?"

"So I understand. I think so."

"Is Lieutenant Williams in love with her?"

"I don't know. I don't think so. No. He likes her."

"He dates her exclusively?"

"Yes."

"He's married?"

"Yes."

"No children."

"That's right, no children."

"He's with her presently in Bangkok, isn't he? Our reports indicate that he's spending a considerable amount of money." Milligan begins to push papers around on his desk. "Lieutenant Stacy, we found certain documents in her bungalow some time ago. Communist propaganda leaflets, etc., directed at colored troops exclusively, describing the American effort in Southeast Asia as a racist, imperialist war, etc." He hands a packet of leaflets across the desk to me. "These."

I take them and shake my head. So Childress really did plant something on her.

"In the next few weeks we're going to have to ask you to remember everything you know about Lieutenant Williams."

I begin to laugh.

"What?" Milligan sits back in his seat. The civilian turns to look at me for the first time.

"This is the stuff that Childress planted on her," I say. "Lieutenant James Childress, before he left for the States."

"I don't understand, young man."

"It was a joke," I say. "Lieutenant Childress planted this stuff in her room to frighten Williams away from her." I uncross my legs and sit back in the chair, confident now that I can clear everything up. "She was his girl first, Childress', and he didn't want Ben—Lieutenant Williams—to have her after he rotated, so he stashed this stuff in her room and called the O.S.I." I start to open the packet which is held together by several rubber bands. I slip one of the bands off the end of the packet. Then I look up and see Colonel Milligan and the civilian staring at each other. "It's a joke," I say. "If you'd known Lieutenant Childress, you'd understand. Ben is no more a communist than you or me."

"Maybe he is and maybe he isn't," the Colonel says. "At any rate it's not a laughing matter," he said sternly.

"We've been investigating the circumstances for a long time, Lieutenant Stacy," the man in civilian clothes says.

"Have you ever wondered where Lieutenant Childress got the leaflets from?" Milligan says.

"Maybe Childress is a communist too," the civilian says, and gets up.

"Maybe they both are," Milligan says.

"Lieutenant Stacy, ex-Lieutenant Childress is in prison in Baltimore now, awaiting trial for killing a policeman." The civilian walks around behind me.

"What?" I turn and look at him. "What?" I look back at Milligan.

Milligan says, "Lieutenant Childress is a black militant, a black racist with the avowed purpose of overthrowing the Government of the United States."

"Goddamn," I say.

"Goddamn, indeed."

"How did it happen?"

"That's why we called you in," the civilian says.

I stare down at the desk. Then I decide to tell them everything I know.

Ben...

The street is silent. I feel almost as if I'm floating through the night air with stoppers in my ears. Everything seems far away. I don't want to think about tomorrow.

The African Star sits on the main street, but farther down, in a quieter section behind a small garden. It is owned by three black ex-GI's who got out of the Army and stayed in Bangkok.

The place looks good, better than I thought it would. I go inside. Warm. A lot of laughter comes from upstairs and I can hear a live jazz band playing. I can tell by the sound that they're black. The downstairs room is about half-full. I find a table, sit down, and order a drink. More music and laughter comes from upstairs whenever the door at the top of the stairs is opened. People come in and go straight upstairs. I wish that I was in the mood for a good party. The noise reminds me of the Hollywood Club in Washington, but the downstairs room of the Hollywood is long, while this room is square and darker.

I remember how the guy at the top of the stairs at the Hollywood would take your dollar and stamp your hand so you wouldn't have to pay again no matter how many times you ran in and out. And we used to do a lot of running between there and Chez Maurice next door, and the Bohemian Caverns around the corner on U Street. Ninth and U Street, or Eleventh and U. Damn, I can't remember, and we used to do it almost every Saturday night when I was stationed at Andrews.

A tall bright-skinned black man comes in the African Star with three Thai girls following him. The bartender knows him. They joke. The bartender is a slender Thai man. The three girls perch on three barstools while the two men talk across the bar.

The bartender digs behind the counter and brings up three packs of black market cigarettes. He gives them to the girls and they slip them in their handbags. The girls sit on the stools and talk among themselves while the two men continue talking. Red slacks, blue slacks, mini-skirt with nice little legs spinning and wiggling.

The bar is made of blue mirrors, and there is a long blue mirror along the wall in back of the row of liquor bottles. A blue ball made of octagonal mirrors spins above the bartender's head.

Several GI's sit with their girls eating soul food in the dim room. The door at the top of the stairs opens. Laughter comes down followed by a round, laughing black GI with a cigar in his mouth. "Hey, Nick, my man," he says as his head emerges out of the stairwell.

"Hey, my man," the tall guy says.

"What's happening?" The black man is wearing a silk suit.

"Nothing."

"Nothing? Man, I thought your name was synonymous with what's happening." He slaps the tall guy on the shoulder.

"Shit, not me."

"Three foxes." He looks at the three girls.

"Friends and cousins of friends," the tall guy says.

"Yeah, how about that."

I listen rather mindlessly to their conversation, happy to be hearing familiar tones and familiar rhythms. A young-looking black man sits at the far end of the bar, drinking by himself. He has long well-shaped sideburns. The waitress brings my scotch and water. I give her a dollar, and she gives me change in baht. I watch her small hands counting out the baht on the tabletop.

"Have you heard the band at the Lido?" the tall guy asks. I begin to drink slowly.

"Where're you from, my man?" a voice very close to my ear says.

I look up and see that it is the young guy from the far end of the bar. "Washington, D. C." I make a sign for him to sit down.

"Greensboro."

"Close."

"Neighbors. What's happening?"

"Nothing."

"Yeah, I know this shit's a bitch. Army?"

"No, Air Force."

"I'm Army, infantry, Vietnam. What're you, in CD?"

"No, I'm a pilot."

He leans back and takes another look. "Oh, shit, a glory boy. Officer."

I laugh.

"Wilton Smith."

"Ben Williams."

"Yeah, so you an officer?"

"I guess."

We sit and talk for a while. The waitress brings two more drinks. "What do you fly?" he asks after a while, as if he has not let the thought out of his mind.

"F-105's."

"That's nice. Super Thuds," he smiles. He drums his fingers on the table for a moment. "I was going to be an officer, but I had to drop out of college—A & T."

"It's not that much difference."

He laughs. "No, man, there's a world of difference. It's a whole different war down in the mud."

"I'm quitting flying anyway," I say to put myself back on equal footing with him.

"Yeah." He drinks slowly. Then he leans back and drums the table. "I haven't been in combat in twenty-one days," he says, as if to put himself ahead of me again. "I been AWOL twenty-one days. I'm not going back. They don't even know where to find me, and if they wait a few more days, I'll be in Sweden somewhere," he whispers as if he trusts me but does not trust the people who might over-hear us. "If you a cop, then you a cop, but I ain't going back. Not alive, I ain't."

"I'm not a cop."

"Well, an officer might be the same thing."

"Shit, man, why would I turn you in?" I say to turn away some of the growing hostility in his manner.

"I don't see why you would go back. They gon' put

your ass in jail. The minute you tell them you ain't gon' kill no more of these people they gon' put you in jail.

"I don't feel like running away."

"I want to live, man," there is rage in his voice now. "I want to live. Shit."

"We been running away long enough," I say angrily.

"*You* been running. I ain't been running nowhere. I was born in the shit and I want a chance to live. That's all. I shot a kid, man. I shot a little Vietnamese kid right in the back, man. The night before I left the 'Nam. I was on patrol in a village near Thuc Yen and this little kid came up to me in an alley and asked me did I want a shoeshine. And sometimes they have bombs in those little boxes. So I told him to set his box down and back off, and he turned and ran, and I shot him right in the back." His voice cracks and he is silent for a moment. "Then I went up and looked in his little box and do you know what I found?"

"I don't know."

"Shoe polish, man. Not a goddamn thing but shoe polish. I went back to base and packed my shit and left. I ain't ever gon' kill no more innocent people, man. And I ain't going to no jail either. I'm still young."

"Okay."

"Not that I'm coming down on you. I thought about the shit too, but if you go to jail, you just as well be dead. Just as well call yourself a dead martyr, and we got enough of them. Don't go to no jail on a bullshit tip, man. I been in jail. You die in jail. There are some Buddhists on Rama One Road near Wat Suthat who can help you get to Japan, and up through Russia to Sweden." He stands up. "I'm going to go back to my hotel," he says. "I didn't mean to come down on you so hard." He laughs. "Ain't your fault that you an officer."

"Good luck," I say as he goes out. I sit down and think about all the black men who have been hitting the road, catching trains. Then I think about all the black men in prisons or on Southern prison farms. I try and weigh one group against another as I pay my check and go out the door.

I go back through the late night streets of Bangkok. I stop at a small all-night coffee shop in the Loom Hotel. I sip the coffee slowly, and think. Then I catch a cab back to our hotel. Damg is asleep when I get there. I turn on the small lamp on the dresser. She is small and beautiful in the dim light. I go into the bathroom and write a note by the small night light above the mirror. Then I pack my things, leave the note and a hundred dollars on the dresser, go out into the hallway and pull the door closed behind me.

WASHINGTON, D.C.

Lionel...

"She's coming back," Fitz says. "God, from the way you're acting, you'd think she's gone forever."

I keep looking out the motel window, which faces north across Washington. The Capitol dome is large and white in the spring sunshine. Fitz continues in the same teasing voice, "You can't control people's fascinations. You got to admit that there is something infinitely fascinating about a big burly nigger looking through the bars of a jail shouting, 'Here come de revolution.' " He giggles.

Out of the corner of my eye I see Fitz fidgeting happily in his chair. I turn and look at him. Until my eyes adjust to the dim light in the room, I see him more as he was six years ago in high school than as he is now. Then slowly I begin to see that in six years his hairline has receded. Now his blond hair starts farther back on his head, giving him an extra inch of skull-smooth forehead to smile with.

"I've been in Washington three years. Three years, Lionel, and the only time you come down to see me is when you have to bring your girl down to see another man, a nigger no less, who is the friend of your girl friend's friend." He lays his head to the side and laughs.

"I swear, Fitz, you ride a joke to death," I say. He sits, cross-legged and small, in striped trousers and a maroon sweater.

"Don't be so tight-assed, Lionel." He uncrosses his legs. "Stop worrying. I lived next door to Roxanne sixteen years of my life. I know her better than you do." He raises his eyebrows, clears his throat and looks at the beds. "Though perhaps not as intimately." His forehead reddens as he smiles.

"Cut it out, Fitz. We slept in separate beds. She's still a virgin."

"Why don't you marry her and be done with it?"

"She promised Stacy that she'd wait."

"She's not going to marry that poor slob." The acne blemishes that covered his cheeks during high school are gone now, leaving his face slightly pitted, in contrast to the smooth skin on his high curved forehead. "I've got a room in Georgetown where I go to get away from the wife when I have to study. Let's go and get drunk, and get you loosened up, for God's sake. You're in love with her, aren't you?"

"I want to marry her."

"As a child Roxanne was always running away. Mrs. Werner would scour the neighborhood calling for her, but Roxie never stayed past suppertime. She has never washed her own dishes or even cleaned her own room in her life. That's why she won't marry Stacy."

I look out the window again. Traffic is noisy outside. It comes out of an underpass and goes up a short hill toward the three-way intersection where Roxanne and I turned off the interstate yesterday.

"And so you haven't been to Washington since we came on the school trip in the fifth grade?"

"Not exactly. I came last year and . . ."

"And you didn't call me." He teases to hide any real disappointment.

"Well, I didn't exactly come to Washington. I flew in to National and went straight to a party in McLean."

"Anyone I know?"

"No, a friend of father's."

"Did Roxanne come?"

"No, Stacy was still here."

"Then you should have called. You could have called. Anyway, we need to toss down a few for old time's sake."

"I want to be here and sober when she comes back."

"We're not going to be that long."

"How far is Baltimore?"

"About forty miles. Did you loan her your car on top of everything?" He laughs.

"No, a colored gal came and picked her up. She was the wife of another friend of Stacy's in Thailand who's run off or something, and they think he's a communist."

"Stacy really knows how to pick them," he says.

"I'd rather stay here, Fitz."

Roxanne...

"If we can get him to write a letter saying he planted the papers on the girl, then your husband will be free of that charge at least," I say to fill the silence with something. She does not answer. She seems to be thinking of something else, but you can't blame her.

I watch the red needle go across the face of the car radio. I turn the knob slowly to unscramble the voices and find some of the kind of music that colored people like. I'm sure now that she doesn't know where her husband is. I lean forward. Sunlight bounces off the bumper of the Volkswagen just ahead of us. The Volkswagen, green, turns off at the exit leading to the Harbor Tunnel.

I think about Childress in the picture he took with Stacy. I see him moving around in his cell like a large caged animal. I don't think he really killed anyone anyway. That's what makes me sick. I know he's sick with bitterness but I bet his face is calm. They just pinned it on him like they do on black men. If I was a black man, they'd probably have something to pin on me. "He didn't really kill the police-man, did he?" I ask quietly.

"Yes."

"Oh." My breath leaves me for a moment. I swallow. "Was it self-defense?"

"I'd rather let him tell you." She sounds annoyed.

I begin to tremble. I wonder if he hates *me*. He has no right to hate *me*. And she's not as friendly as colored people usually are. She's smaller than I thought she'd be, and pret-tier. "I don't see how you can be so calm. If I were you I'd be tearing my hair out. Every congressman in Washington would know about my husband by now."

"Unh," she says. She does not look at me and soon she has retreated again to what she had been thinking about be-fore. She bites the corner of her lip.

I look out the window. A low green sign reads BALTI-MORE 8. "I think the war is stupid anyway. They're just wasting American boys for nothing." The sign goes past. "I wish that Stacy had decided not to fly, too. We could live in Sweden somewhere. How long have you been married?"

"Two years."

"Stacy and I are going to get married as soon as he gets back." The tires begin to click over the seams in the con-crete. I wonder what she is thinking of me. I'm tired of won-dering what people think of me, doggone it. I've got to live my own life, and I've got to do some of the things that I want to do. I didn't make her come with me. I asked her to come, and she made up her own mind. She knows Childress better than she wants to let on. "Where is Childress from?" I ask.

"Texas. He went to college for a couple of years in Baltimore. That's why he came back to Baltimore after the war, but he's from Texas."

I look at her. I never hated them. I used to feel sorry for colored girls. In the fifth grade I thanked God that I was not one of them, born like that, with hair like that, like Marva Tittle's that used to stick out whenever she played. In high school I used to feel so sorry for her. She was the only colored person in the school, and the white boys used to get her to do-it by telling her that they would take her to the prom or something. And then sometimes three or four of them would take her out and make her do-it and they would come back and laugh at her.

I wonder did Stacy ever get her. If he did, he went alone, and afterward he suppressed the fact so deep that he could still think of himself as a virgin. I wonder did he? I don't even think he would know.

I can see the skyline of Baltimore come into sight. I know what he's going to think. Maybe he wouldn't find out. I look out the window at the gravel along the side of the road. He doesn't own me. You can't just give up your life just because someone else can't be secure unless he owns you.

I got my own life to live. She lives her own life. If I get into trouble, then I have to get myself out.

"What's he like?" I ask.

"Bitter. Arrogant. I don't know."

"You been to see him before?"

"Twice. He was a friend of Ben's, I thought."

"That was before you learned about the papers, huh?"

"The first time I heard about them was when you called."

"I called as soon as Stacy wrote me. I rushed down here to see if there was anything I could do to help. Stacy doesn't even know I came down."

She looks at me with an expression that said, I bet he doesn't. I stop looking at her.

Rose...

She's a nuisance more than anything, I think, sitting
there in the small room. Now that we're here I wish I
could've come alone. I wish I could talk to Childress alone.
I'd like to slap his face.

I wonder why he had to come back to America and lie
to me. There were millions of other women he could've lied
to. And I like a fool let him touch me. I even thought I loved
him once, like a fool. I feel like sitting in a tub of scalding
hot water and washing every part of me that he ever put his
dirty hands on.

The guard comes back again with his round butt.
Sometimes Negroes make me sick. He thinks he's cute with
his little old mustache, but he'd stop strutting back and
forth across here if he knew that wasn't nobody paying attention to him.

He probably wants Roxanne to see him. He probably
thinks that any white girl hanging out with a colored girl is
looking for black men. I look at the floor. His shoes are shiny

against the green tile. I sit back on the sofa and wait for the other guard, the white ugly one, to quit wasting time. She's a nuisance more than anything, I think.

I wonder why Childress did it. The white guard beckons for us to come up and sign the book. I pick up my driver's license and Civil Service ID card from the counter. He takes them again and compares the signature I put on the book to the signature on the cards. Then he looks at me and looks at the photograph on my driver's license.

Roxanne signs the book. He looks at her driver's license. Then he looks at the photograph on her college ID card and up at her. I put my cards back in my purse. We go back and sit down. The black guard walks across in front of us again. The jail smells of pine oil disinfectant, which does not quite cover the odor of human mustiness. A steel door slams closed down the hallway. I exhale deeply, tired of waiting.

"How long do they make you wait?" she says.

"Forever, sometimes. I don't know," I say.

"How does he look?"

"Same as . . ." I shrug. She makes me sick with her stupid questions. I sit for a minute, waiting for her to say something else. When she doesn't, I begin to think about Childress again. For a moment I am glad that they have him in jail. Then I stop myself from thinking that. No.

I'm glad that Ben decided not to fly any more. I'm glad. He don't need to be over there anyway, fighting them people.

I feel myself getting nervous, shaking. There are so many things that can't be undone. Another guard comes and leads us down the hallway. He is tall, and he walks wide-legged. We go into the room where they will bring Childress. A heavyset white woman comes in and searches us. Then the guard takes our handbags and staples them inside a large paper bag and puts them on a chair. We go up to the steel wire and sit.

"Which way will they bring him in?" she says.

"Through that door," I say. The door swings open and a guard comes out, closing it behind him. Roxanne pushes the hair back from the side of her face and looks at me.

Ben shouldn't have been over there in the first place. Maybe he should've played like he was crazy. If they'd given him a bad discharge, we could still've lived on what I make. Out of what I make we could've saved enough to make a down payment on a house. We could've gone back to North Carolina, where he might have been able to teach school without anyone asking about his discharge. Especially after he got a little older.

You can't beat these crackers, I think. They got so many ways to beat you, and they got so many Negroes that will help them.

I went to his apartment the first night, like a fool, because there was no one at home for me to talk to, and I didn't want to go back there to stare at the four walls. So I just went with him like a fool. The apartment was nice, on a high floor. We could see the skyline of Baltimore through the picture window.

He laid his hands on me and I said, "I don't think we should, Childress." The music from the stereo was nice. It came up in the silence between my words. "I'm married, Childress. You know I'm married."

I moved away from him across the soft rug and began looking at the design on the Oriental room divider.

He smiled like he wasn't even hearing me. I went back to the picture window and looked out at the lights. Soon he put a glass of scotch on the window sill. He turned me around and I let him kiss me.

His hands were large against my back. And later he seemed large because it had been a long time since I had been with a man. He hurt me a little, but more than that I couldn't get my mind off of Ben until I started to like it, and there was something about Childress that is hard to deny.

He doesn't force his way into your personal life like Ben does.

His back was smooth and broad under my hands and I could hold him nice, just spread my hands across his back and hold him. And he felt good and strong. I finished and felt good.

I don't think he even noticed or cared until he was finished. I was happy. I didn't even think about the possibility of getting pregnant. I just wanted to lay there against him while he was off somewhere minding his own business.

And for almost a month I almost never thought about Ben. I used to go to Baltimore about twice a week, and drive the forty miles home by myself without even thinking about Ben.

Childress...

She stares at me hatefully through the heavy wire screen that separates me from them. Then she sits forward in her chair. "No, I don't see why you did it."

"Rose, I already told you I was wrong. I'm sorry. What can I say?" I scoot the chair forward. The legs scrape on the tile floor.

"But why? That's what I don't understand."

"I told you, I don't know. I already explained to the FBI that I put the stuff on the girl. What else can I do? You talk like he's going to have that hanging over his head all his life. The only thing he really got to worry about is what he did to himself."

She drops her head. After a moment of silence I can tell that she has started to think about the things we did, about how I lied to her. "I'm sorry, baby." She doesn't look up at me. I look at the white girl. "How's Stacy?"

"He's fine," she says.

"How many more does he have?" I shift a little so I can

see her clearly through the screen. She's not as pretty as Stacy made her out to be, but she's pretty. A little skinny.

"Seventeen, the last letter said."

"One month if the weather holds."

"I guess. How are you doing?"

"I'm in here. I couldn't be doing too well," I say. I look back at Rose to see if she has cooled off and is ready to listen. I shift a little so I can see her face better. "I'm sorry that ya'll had to come under these circumstances, because I really wanted to talk to some friendly people." I smile.

The strongest light comes from the window behind me. It casts the shadow of the screen across their faces. "I told the FBI all I knew. I swear."

"What they want to know, Stacy said, is where you got the papers from," the white girl says.

"It was my stuff. I used to read stuff like that. I got it in Hong Kong." I look at Rose. "I explained all that. Rose, I was looking for answers too, just like everyone else. Everyone thought I knew all the answers, because I seemed so sure of myself, but I was searching like a lot of other people. That part is true, Rose. I swear."

"What happened?" the white girl asks.

"I killed a cop."

"I mean, did you really kill him?"

"Yeah."

She swallows hard. "How, Lieutenant Childress?"

"I don't know. I was walking down the street in Baltimore in the middle of the day and this young black dude was handing out leaflets on the corner. So I took one and started to read it. Then this big ugly white cop come up and told me to get moving, like that. So I told him to wait a minute until I finish reading my little leaflet. And he said, 'Get your black ass moving. *Now.*' I said, 'Man, I got a Constitutional right to be here just like everybody else.' And the sucker draws his pistol and tells me, 'This is all the Constitution you need.' So I go to get in my car, and when I started to get in, the cracker kicked me dead in my ass. So, I picked up a jack handle and knocked the gun out of his hand and knocked him down. He killed his own damn self when his head hit the concrete. All I was trying to do is teach him not to kick anybody any more. I tried to tear his leg off."

"He kicked you first," Rose says.

"That's still not self-defense, Rose."

"I know, but I don't care."

The white girl is silent. She's not as pretty as Stacy made her out to be. A little too skinny, no titties. Splotchy-skinned, but not bad. It's hard to tell if her teeth are dingy since her skin is so light.

"But I did love you, Rose," I say.

"I wish you'd never found me, Childress. You didn't have to come up under me lying."

"I'm sorry."

"When will you get out?" the white girl asks.

"Maybe next year. Maybe never. I don't think they mean to let me out. One-hundred-thousand-dollars bail. My folks are trying to raise it, but I don't think they will."

"I'd like to help," the white girl says. "Maybe I can help."

I look at her for a long time. "Okay, if you can do something, do it."

"I can try," she says.

THAILAND

Stacy...

Childress will fuck her. I know he will.

I open my eyes and think about Lionel's letter again. Even if I could leave now I could not get there in time to stop it. I stare up at the canvas and think again that it is not funny to say it that way, but I can't stop saying it that way. All night I was saying it over in my mind that way: If you extend yourself too far, you can't protect your flanks. The thought of them being together makes chills run through me.

I lay still and listen to the screaming of the jet engines down on the test pad.

Even if I could steal a plane and start now, I couldn't get there on time. I'd run out of gas before I could get there. I'd run out of gas somewhere northeast of Guam.

I think about the thousands of miles of empty air between here and Baltimore. I think about time, and how we should have invented a machine that you could get into and be in Baltimore almost at the same moment. I stiffen my body and bite my lip and wonder whether it could be done. Necessity is the mother of invention. Necessity is the mother of invention.

I wonder why she had to go down there at all in the first place.

She knows how he is. I wrote her things about him. I grinned while I wrote her: He spent a weekend with two whores at Pattaya. He screwed the colonel's wife at Nellis. He had a lot of funny things to say about the difference between black women, white women and yellow women. I used to invent things to tell her about the way he is, just to have a little fun.

I think about them together for a while. Then I get up slowly and put my bathrobe around me. The first waves of daytime heat come down off the dusty canvas above me. I get my toothbrush and facecloth from the locker. The locker door clangs closed. I walk out of the tent with my towel across my arm. The screen door slams shut. The sand is soft under foot. It is already beginning to heat up. I think about her. Selfish, whining, self-pitying.

The stairs to the bathhouse are shaky under me. I push the door open. Someone is under the shower. I ignore whoever it is and go past and put my towel on the shelf above the third face bowl. I look in the mirror, then splash cold water up into my face, then look up at myself again.

Where do I have to fly today? My eyes look tired. I don't want to fly. But I'd go crazy if I had to stay on the ground all day, thinking. I brush my teeth and gargle with clean water. Skin. I need a shave. I hate to put the oxygen mask on unless I have shaved.

Captain Windgate comes out of the shower stall whistling, the idiot. "You ready to go monkey-hunting?" he says, with his stupid face smiling.

"I guess," I say, and smile.

"How many more you got?"

"Ten," I say. He dries himself. He props his foot on a face bowl while he dries his leg. There is a dimple at the side of his ass. He lifts the other leg and dries it. I see his penis hanging. Pink.

"I'll be glad when this entire fucking thing is over," he says.

I gargle with cold water again so I won't have to answer him. I take off my robe and go into the shower. When I come out, the showerhouse is empty. I go down the stairs into the sand. The sun throws long shadows across me. I begin to wish that Childress had been killed in action. That would have solved everything. I think about them being together and have to stop walking for a moment.

"Hey, I hope you haven't been there all night," Bordreau says. He is coming from another showerhouse. "I pissed on something in exactly that spot last night. I thought it was a tree."

"It was me," I say, and laugh. I twist my towel and snap at his naked behind. He runs a few steps.

"Sorry about that." He giggles.

He and Childress are the only ones in the outfit who walked from the tents to the showerhouses naked. Bordreau runs on the ball and heel of his feet back between the first row of tents.

Maybe Childress *is* a communist, I think.

Lieutenant Colonel Milligan...

We know all that, we know all that, goddamnit, Peterson. I can look around the briefing room and see that the troops are in a hurry to get started. We could do away with half of this happy horseshit, and by God, if I were wing commander we would.

The room is dark, but you can feel when a bunch of young troops are restless and ready to go, and a briefing officer can dampen their spirits just like a bad football coach. Shit.

Peterson says, "And *do not* overfly ships of any foreign nation in Haiphong Harbor, be they Russian, Chinese or whatever. *Do not* overfly the center of Hanoi. In the gulf, *do not* turn inbound to Hainan Island. The call-sign for the

Navy is Roscoe." Peterson leans in and out of the podium light. The briefing map is lighted behind him with all the restricted areas clearly outlined in Day-Glo paints.

"Lieutenant Peterson, we have a takeoff time to meet," I say.

"Roger, sir, just a few more items to cover," he says as he blinks behind his glasses. Rather than waste time arguing with him, I decide to hear the items out.

Bordreau...

I ought to taxi over the fool, I think. I push my throttles forward, but hold my parking brakes and lean forward in the cockpit. Hot. I can't do what I am supposed to do for watching that fool. Smoke from the engine of the plane ahead of me comes back across my windscreen. I push my oxygen mask up.

He steps out on the grass to get around the plane ahead of me, then he comes back on the concrete surface of the arming pad. I lean to the side and look at him walk up beside me with his tennis shoes on and a white silk cowl draped around the shoulders of his flight fatigues. He throws holy water on the nose of my plane, blessing me, the fool. And to think, they gave him a Bronze Star just for volunteering to stay over here an extra tour.

Lieutenant Colonel Milligan...

The air above the cloud blanket is smooth. I tell the spares that they can turn around and go home because all the strike aircraft seem to be doing well. I look back over my shoulder and see them peel off and start back. Then the radios are silent as we press on. I still haven't decided what to do, I think. I look down at the cloud blanket, moving slowly below us. I fidget in my seat. The parachute harness is tight between my legs.

If you want to get the job done, I think, then you've got to break a few ironclad rules enforced by the rigidity of bureaucratic thinking at higher headquarter levels.

I look down and curse the clouds. They could have made it so easy just by not being there. I can tell by the texture of the clouds that we're approaching the gulf, where the white billows will turn into gray patchy scud. The scud is about fifty miles ahead of us.

Damn. It's the commander in the field who makes the last-minute decisions that save ninety percent of the missions from failure. So I've got the ball. What do I do, run or punt?

I look at my ground-speed indicator. Then I look down again and wonder should I take the force down below the clouds and take a chance of getting clobbered when we come back in over land.

Not a break. Nothing. We have to get down before we get out over water. Fifty miles. No matter what I decide, there'll be troops flying behind me who will disagree with the decision. Especially if we take losses, which we will. Some of us will get clobbered down there. But you don't discover something like the splash technique, for example, which will save lives in the long run, by being unwilling to violate some of the tried-and-true formulas that lead to a high percentage of mediocre successes but few meaningful blows against the enemy.

I look eastward toward Phuc Yen and wonder if the Migs have room to get off the ground beneath the undercast. For all I know they might be waiting for us to crack the deck. The guns might be waiting. I make a shallow turn to keep the force together. Some of the birds are heavier than I am.

The weather scout says, "It's solid down to five thousand. Tops about seven thousand."

"Roger, Tall Cotton, Rain Dancer lead, I copied five and seven," I say. Two thousand feet thick, I think. The clouds are thick enough for Migs to be loitering inside them. I check my fuel gauges. I wish that Chappy was here to pray for us now. I look down. Those who value freedom have to be willing to gamble to defend it. If you succeed, the risk, the losses, were worth it, and you get a nice pat on the back. If you fail you can kiss your career good-by. And you have the difficult task of notifying a man's wife that her husband has been shot down and captured, or else blown to bits. But we've got to go down, I decide.

Stacy...

We drop down below the cloud deck. The last hills slope away beneath us as we fly straight for the coastline. The land is spread out beneath us, wet and marshy below the scud. All that I can hear is the sound of my airplane whistling through the air, seemingly far away, made to seem far away by the silent seashell roaring of the cup of my earphone. And then sometimes I hear myself drawing oxygen hard from within my face mask. And sometimes a side tone comes over the radio, but no one speaks. I wonder who it is. I wonder if they are waiting for us.

The wet silence is eerie. Over water the solid overcast breaks up into gray patchy clouds that let in some of the light from the sky above.

We start a turn. I fall in behind Bookbinder 2 and throttle back to get spacing for the run. I lose altitude for a moment. Then I bring it up. We stay in the turn until the shoreline is directly off the nose. I think about Childress and her together. I look north to Haiphong Harbor. It is full of ships of the nations that are supposed to be our friends. I stare at the flags. Nations that begged us for help during the Second World War now trading with people who hate us, selling them guns and ammunitions that they will use against us, or against some poor American grunt, slogging around in the mud down south. That kind of thing is disgusting. The ships are backed out into the middle of the inlet, waiting to get to the docks to unload.

I'd like to blow one of the damn ships out of the water. Nations with flags the same color as ours. The Dutch, the British, the French, and we helped the damn French fight this same damn war for two decades. I look at them and feel like the bottom of the world has opened up and we are flying across the mouth of the deep wide pit alone. I think about Roxanne. Maybe Childress *is* a communist. I watch the wing tips of Bookbinder 2 to see if he is going to make any more course corrections.

The defending guns are still silent as Rain Dancer's flight begins strafing the floor of the valley. Then the radios begin: "Radar, this is Rain Dancer 1, they're still playing possum. Keep the second flight at the same altitude."

"Roger, Maverick flight copies. Maybe we'll try something heavier."

"Roger, we're breaking left and coming back across south of the ingress track."

Sometimes they fight and sometimes they run away before you get there, or they lay and wait until they've got a fat one picked out and they open up with everything they got. I squint and see a long line of huts and one large storage building light up as Maverick flight lays down some three-thousand-pounders.

"Radar, keep your eyes out for Migs," someone says. "Roger."

There are a million excuses you can give for not getting the job done, I think. But it all boils down to the fact that you either get it done or you don't. And when the odds are stacked against you, that's all the more reason why you have to clench your fist and grit your teeth. And if you have to sink the whole damn continent into the ocean, then you sink the whole damn continent.

Pink Plum flight breaks off and climbs to the left to wait for the guns to open up so he can come across and take them out before someone gets hit.

I drop my nose. The red pip of my cannonsight climbs slowly to the firing position. I watch it. I see a line of trucks camouflaged against a row of huts. I steady the pip and squeeze the trigger as I streak downward. It's the goddamn Jews and women who are betraying the white race. I think about Childress and Roxanne in bed together. My firing jolts me and I seem to hang for a moment, while the backward thrust of the guns battles the forward push of the engines.

Then the whole wet floor of the valley lights up, and white puffs of thirty-seven-millimeter gunfire explodes like popcorn in the wet air. "They're home all right, and expecting company," someone jokes.

"I'm hit, I'm hit, radar. I'm heading for the water."

"Who's hit? Give your call-sign!"

"Spinnet 3, damnit. They got me twice. Am I on fire?"

"Negative. This is Spinnet 4. I'm right behind you. Take it easy. You're smoking. You're getting some drainage."

I turn short of the hills and look back across the valley,

which looks like firecrackers have been strewn across the ground. After the last plane comes across, the guns fall silent again and the land is still, except for the fires we have started. I think civilization itself is in danger right here in the mud of Vietnam and you've got to fight even if no one else wants to help. The world is full of Gooks and niggers and they'll tear down everything the white man has ever built, I say to myself, almost as if I am talking to Roxanne, not to get her to agree with me, but just so she has it for the record. I wouldn't touch her now with a ten-foot pole. I don't want to come within miles of her. She's never even going to know where I am. I hope there's a lying letter from her waiting when I get back, so I can tear it up.

If she's still in Baltimore, she wouldn't mail the letter. Or maybe she and Childress would ride all the way to New York so it would have a New York postmark. But it would have happened four or five days ago for the letter to be there when I get down, and it would have been weeks ago that she went to Baltimore in the first place. I didn't even look at the postmark on Lionel's letter.

He should've been over here fighting for the country just like everybody else. "Missile up, SAM launch," Navy radar says. I shudder, and look in front of me for the big red-and-white telephone pole that, if it explodes within a few feet of you, can knock you out of the air.

"Pink Plum, did you see the launch location?"

"Roger, I'll see if I can't burn them out of there."

"Aircraft clear," radar says.

I lean back in my seat and begin to breathe again. They would love it if I got shot down. They would pretend to be sad for me in bed together. We go down for another pass.

The valley floor becomes a mass of sparkling gun barrels again.

"Can you make the water, Spinnet 3?" radar says on common frequency.

"I'm over water. I'm bailing out." His voice is shaky.

I hear the beep, beep, beep of his parachute beeper. I have to turn my radio down for a moment. We turn out over water and I see his parachute billow out in the wind below us. I watch him down. The guns across the valley are silent again as the last planes streak out of the valley. My forehead is running water like a faucet.

I clamp my lips together. You honor your commitments. You don't sit around pissing in your pants, crying about what someone has done to you. You fix them so they can't ever do it again. You fight until there's nothing left in you to fight with, by God. You vanquish the foe and you have Pax Romana, as Colonel Holland used to say in flight school, and then you're safe for a thousand years.

We should never have brought them to America, or we should have sent them back after the Civil War. I think about that. The thought warms me. All this wouldn't've happened. I waited for five years for Roxanne's and my wedding night. Like you save a piece of candy, like you store away something for yourself. I stare out the windscreen, wishing it could have happened that way.

I slam my three-thousand-pounder against the side of a building. It impacts in an area where a secondary fire is already burning. And since the guns are still silent we come across again. I roll upside-down, and after I get over the same building I let my nose fall through and lob another six-hundred-pounder into the thick. I lean on the right rudder and streak off behind Bookbinder 2. We hug the trees at the head of the valley and wait for the guns. The smoke from the fires does not spiral too high in the wet air.

All the old virtues. Courage and will-power and perse-verance—you depend on them when there's nothing else. And perspiration. My entire back is wet with sweat.

"Roger, Tomahawk, come left, come left," Navy radar says.

"Hello. I wish the bastards would shoot so we could pinpoint them. Okay, radar, I'm coming to the left. What do you see?"

"The black smoke looks like oil burning. Maybe you can light it up a little more."

"Roger, I see it."

"Roger, off your nose, Bookbinder, do you have Toma-hawk in sight?"

"Negative," our lead says.

"Come right to zero-nine-five. He'll be off your nose low."

"Roger, I have the four Tomahawk aircraft."

"Roger, can you make a flight of eight and give Toma-hawk a hand?"

I hear Spinnet 3's beeper on the water far away. We whistle downward at such an angle that I have nothing but a vista of the valley spread across my windshield. The wrong people are always the ones who get killed. I can almost stand aside and see my own death as we go down. I can al-most feel the thump that is like no other thump in the world, and then I can almost feel the heat before the fire gets to the tanks. My hands sweat on the trigger of the ejec-tion seat, but for some reason I pause, then I can almost feel the explosion hit like a sledge hammer in my back. I see the flash for an instant before everything goes black, and I can see the wreckage of my plane, twirling earthward and hitting the wet floor of the valley, which we have already saturated with fire.

WASHINGTON, D.C.

Rose...

I don't know whether I would want Ben to come back.
I don't know. There is something about Ben that I love, like
I would love if Ben had given me a child and the child
would have been just like him. That would have been nice.

I wonder what will happen to him.

I walk down the street with my face set. The sun is
nice. The sidewalk is crowded. Maybe I can go and see Ben
when he turns up. I would like to see old Ben. I smile, thinking about it. Then I begin to worry again.

I go into the building. Calvin is waiting in the hallway
with a leather suit on.

"Got your mouth poked out this morning," he says as
we get on the elevator. "Didn't even want to get up this
morning, did you?"

"This is my natural expression, like it or not." The elevator starts to go up.

He throws up his hands, "Okay, sister." He laughs.
Then he hugs me.

I think I am going to save my money. And old Ben will get in touch with me sooner or later. And I think I'd like to go and see his old black self. I smile, and old Calvin thinks I am smiling at him. I know one thing, with Ben it's only a matter of time until he gets a message to me some kind of way. That's the way he is.

About the Author

GEORGE DAVIS was born in West Virginia, and reared in a half dozen small towns in Virginia, West Virginia, and Maryland. He is a graduate of Colgate University, and holds a Master of Fine Arts degree from Columbia. He has worked as a staff writer and editor for the *Washington Post* and as a deskman for the New York Times Sunday Department. His fiction has appeared in *Black World*, *Black Review*, and *Amistad 1*. During 1967 and 1968, he flew forty-seven combat missions over Vietnam and Laos as a navigator with the United States Air Force, earning an Air Medal, and a nomination for a Distinguished Flying Cross. He is a member of the John O. Killens Writers' Workshop at Columbia University.